There is little to tell y[ou].
I am by nature solitar[y, un]
happy, very morose. I loathe books and never read
them. Except informative books, giving me facts,
any facts and all facts. I love travel best of all, and
yet get very impatient with it. I like walking. I like
talking. I love meeting people once. I love best
knowing absolutely no one: but watching every
one. I dislike having to live in London, a parochial
little village. But I have to. I dislike it so much, that
it does me (creatively) an awful lot of good. It's the
pearl in my oyster. I dislike things very thoroughly
indeed. Otherwise (I live in London, Eng) one gets
genteel, tea shoppe, bored, refined, amateurish.
All things which make it so difficult for the creative
artist to live in England, which is secure, pleasant,
imitative, watery...

(from an autobiographical entry by Olive Moore in
the 1933 edition of *Authors Today and Yesterday*)

Other titles in the
Extraordinary Classics series

A Brief Life
Juan Carlos Onetti

The Shipyard
Juan Carlos Onetti

The Book of Disquiet
Fernando Pessoa

The Walk
Robert Walser

❧ FUGUE
Olive Moore

SERPENT'S
TAIL

Series editors: Pete Ayrton and Martin Chalmers

Library of Congress Catalog Card Number: 92-83756

A CIP catalogue record for this book is available from the British Library on request

Copyright © 1932 the Estate of Constance Vaughan

First published in 1932 by Jarrolds Publishers, London

This edition published in 1993 by Serpent's Tail,
4 Blackstock Mews, London N4
and 401 West Broadway #1, New York, NY 10012

Printed in Finland by Werner Söderström Oy

Per il che si ha a notare, che gli uomini si debbono o vezzegiare o spegnere. . . .

MACHIAVELLI

(*Il Principe*, Capitolo III: "De' principati misti")

A night to lead minor poets down white roads to the sea. He hurried over the network of cobbles, keeping close to houses so angular with age as to seem but the reflection of themselves in dark water. From its flute the fountain played a watery tune. Despite his cautious step the stones rang with a hard deliberate malice as though to give warning of his escape; yet he hurried on, down twists and turnings that led an irregular and unwilling way to the narrow river, to the Raben Tor, to the road beyond the ramparts.

On the bridge he paused, thinking not without humour that where others took such pains to outdistance enemies, his haste was but to escape from friends.

The river was like a live thinking mirror. On its surface trailed a luminous finger. Infinitely deep, chill, and distant it seemed, gathered in heavy soundless movement under the cold lunar fingering. Incredible that an accent of light should work such distortion on a face which by day was friendly and shining, passing through the village from the fields over reeds and brown pebbles and the shouting children's naked feet; the women kneeling at its rim slapping the shirts and linen in a passionate ritual of duty and cleanliness, to which the younger women sang and the old cackled with a certain featherless busyness.

But this was no moment to idle on bridges. He must get beyond the village, through the Raben Tor, and out to the lane between the vines, leading to the hills.

He had escaped the crowded room but not its memory. Still through the fog of tobacco smoke Madame's pomeranian, rat-eyed, rat-faced, a dog like an ugly and spoiled child, yap-yapped for sugar and attention; the few peasants at the far end of the Wynstub chuckled over their cards and called the score in their hearty Alsatian speech which is like having one's mouth full of *The Canterbury Tales;* and Simeon Fenn, the elegant and out-of-place, leaned his head against the wall not taking his eyes from

Lorwich's face, to whom Otto was explaining: first we had the old French taxes, then came the German, and now come the new French taxes, and we pay all three. Can you blame the Autonomists?

—O wine, wine! cried Sebastian. Fertiliser of the mind! Aphrodisiac of the soul! (Lend me your pencil, Lavinia. I'll write that down.)

A querulous voice was refusing to believe that the marriage of D'Arcy and Elizabeth was ever consummated. And the impersonal sweating Karl of the round red face and uncomprehending blue eye, swung his jugs and bottles through the confusion of smoke and people. Place your Italian on the soil, Christopher Lorwich was saying, and you have placed him rightly. Sow Italy with salt and the Italian will prove as undying as the Jew. You will find him in every corner of the earth keeping his albergo, making his wine and pasta, building the world's roads, digging the earth and seeing that there is fruit from it. He has that deathless sense of race and family.

Miss Reade was complaining to Otto that there was nothing, nothing, in the *Guides Bleus* but *guerre sanglante* and *une très belle église moderne*.

—So that now the only thing to do is to jump on Russia. (The portly French doctor having missed the last train back to Strasbourg, was gathering his short fingers in little bunches and shaking them. His voice was live and quarrelsome.) Then Russia is off: finished. And so are the hotheads and the two to four million unemployed wandering about in every country and making a cursed nuisance of themselves. So long as they ate up their own savings it was bearable. (The doctor smiled.) But now they would eat up ours. They menace. They dare to threaten. Our answer must be to get rid of them. So long as they leave us in peace what can it matter how many heads they break: or whose? And what can it matter to us how savagely they annihilate one another so long as they do it thoroughly and in the name of Honour, Liberty, and Truth?

—(O nectarous, O pellucid beer! sighed Sebastian. From thy foam how many an Aphrodite has been born!)

—And do not think that England will escape. (The doctor was growing angry with Lorwich.) Yes, yes: we know it cannot be. Nothing ever can be, where the English are concerned. The world will continue to be the Englishman's little ball, and he to be the modern Atlas carrying his golf-clubs on his back. But slowly, imperceptibly, it will happen, my friend, even to you. You English do all things slowly. You will be atheists and communists without having noticed it or knowing how it happened to you, and without having shed one drop of blood. You English evolve so slowly. You do not believe me? But why should you doubt? Did not Darwin evolve an Englishman out of a monkey?

A sharp and prolonged clapping as though the gods themselves approved came loudly from the skies.

—The storks! The storks! cried Miss Reade. The storks are back! And leaned from the window to watch them settle. It was then (with her back to him) that he had turned to see if the door were open, and with hardly a sound had stood up to make his escape. But Sebastian had seen him (trust Sebastian) and with a lewd and intimate leer had twisted his owlish face in a drunken wink; so that for a fraction of a second he had hesitated, impaled, as it were, on Sebastian's knowing wink; unsure whether to go forward or retreat and coldly angry with himself for trying to appear to be leaving the room unnoticed for a purpose.

And here he was already above the village. He looked down on it, warm within its walls and guarded by the three squat gates with their high conic towers.

How astrologic the gothic! Made at night, can one doubt?, by searching the skies. The huddled houses upheld each other like a troupe of mediæval beggars. Above them the swaying roofs advanced and retreated: those sweeping Alsatian roofs, argus-eyed. And at the corners the serene octagonal fountains piped their reedy tune. How cold and sufficient their slow measure. How distant Italy and the baroque, with its tyranny of prancing Tritons. How sober and how unsteady it all was. A sober fact told by a wavering tongue: the potato grafted to the vine.

She would come and look for him. Of that he had no doubt. When she had turned and found him gone and Sebastian had rounded off the wink with the witty remark. She would sit down and talk brightly and quickly about nothing at all, and then jump up snatching at her book and handbag. Sebastian would again be beerily facetious. Obsessed by her one thought she would not resent it. Probably she would laugh. She had no pride. Of course she would laugh, snatching her bag and book without pretence, and hurrying away. And what was the use of remonstrating with her? She had the ruthless and irritating logic of the child. She would probably say, greatly surprised: Well, why did you run away?

Or she would say, as she had often said: Pride. *Pride?* Surely one can always put *that* down and pick it up again.

Except that she never picked it up again; or so it seemed. I am. I want. I must. I will. And she would find him here. She would take the road he had taken with an instinct as sure as though she had placed her nose to the ground. She would stand where he stood now; and he would be treated to the small boy running away from his nurse, or the heartless trifler with outraged love. It would depend on her mood. And from the moment he had got outside the house, no, from the moment he had got up from the table, he had known she would pursue and overtake. One would have to run a little further than the Raben Tor to escape Lavinia Reade!

Even so it was foolish to place himself deliberately in her path, so he climbed the bank beside the road and continued walking, hidden by the vines spread in long orderly rows on the hill-side. He was aware of the lush dark green smell of evening and of the metallic ring the vineleaves gave as they brushed past him; and, now, that the dark shape he had taken vaguely for someone approaching was but the Christ marking the boundary of another vineyard.

They were at every corner these Crosses, bearing their gaunt and sorrowing burdens. They were mostly worn and moss-grown; but here and there were newly painted in the gay toy-soldiery of scarlet and gold, looking for a while almost happy. But always wrong; always out of place. Their surroundings mocked and cast them off, this sudden frown on a pleasant face. The very air of the hills and the grins on the flat kind faces of the people called for a tippler and a wineskin, or Omar and his book and bottle, or the jovial Hotei and his shaking belly. But only row upon row of gaunt Christs sunning themselves at the corners of the vineyards and looking unutterably sad and tired and foolish.

In the evening light, detail-less, simplified to the intention, the Christ had an impressive and mournful dignity. In the night the field was His. The vines, their arms upheld, no longer mocked the tyranny of His obstinate and abiding melancholy. He hung there, absolute in loneliness, turning aside His drooping head.

O crux ave spes unica!

Harrion was near enough now to make out the larger words and also the date

1643

**Gedenke, O Herr... von diesem Kreuze...
reumuthig... glauben betet... erlangt...**

Forty days Grace promised for four Our Fathers and five Hail Marys said kneeling at this spot. A long chain-letter to have started three hundred years since! He studied the averted head and hungry arms and looked down again at the moss-obliterated words. He ground the earth with the toe of his shoe, and felt himself growing angry. Yet he had passed it a hundred times and had no feelings on the subject. But now he could feel as something physical the slow anger rising up in him. God! do we not all die for our fellow-men? What is it all but a daily death for others? Do we not all stretch hungry arms and avert our faces; betray and accept betrayal; and light our indestructible little souls along the everlasting road—though Time itself prove but a moment in Eternity?

—*O please* (with curious precision he recalled the glee it had given him as a child to stammer his wicked and unfailing joke) O *please* don't cleave the Rock of Ages for *me!* And the slow colour darkening his mother's face that Sunday afternoon on which he had suddenly put down his spoon and fork and said seriously and with his mouth full: Well, I *do* think Jesus is conceited saying I am the Light of the World.

This consuming anger, this hatred possessing him a moment since: he who had finished with anger and such passionate beliefs. In the cold averted face the red colour darkened, and the hungry unloved arms, powerless at last, reached out to him.

But here came Miss Reade. Knowing that from where he stood she could not see him, he did not move and watched her as she came slowly and with a small hesitant step, keeping well to the middle of the road. Evidently she was not at ease wandering alone at so late an hour of the night. But he was neither sorry for her, nor angry, nor amused, but watched her as though he had not seen her before; impersonally, as one watches unseen a person unknown to one. And she came as though led to the foot of the slope from which he watched her, and stopped dead. She was looking beyond the village, down across the plain, where at set distances other such villages glowed like tight bunches of dark heather, and a few lights shone. She turned her head to look down the road she had come, and then back again following it into the distance.

It was no use going any further. There was no-one. She had mistaken the road, after all. Yet she stood there undecided, unwilling to admit defeat, and peered on into the distance. And all at once she raised her head in an abrupt defiant jerk and stared at the sky. She stood alone and without movement, staring long and steadily at the stars as though wondering to what conclusions they had come. By their light her face took on a luminous unreal surface-quality of stone. The glitter in her eye might have been tears. Then she looked down again; her face set and expressionless. She stared at her feet, and once more down the road, and then with an impatient movement turned on her heel and went back the way she had come.

He saw her smaller, smaller, and lost in shadow. But if one is indifferent one can at least be good-mannered. Why should he have deprived her of her triumph. What did it matter to him now whether she found him or not: and how greatly it mattered to her, this tall undaunted creature who carried his child inside her. The least he could do, Harrion decided, was to overtake her in the village and let her lead him back, obedient to heel, up the steps Zum Goldenen Lamm.

By taking the footpath instead of the road he was first in the village, and they met in a side street leading to the bridge. She walked past him, her head high. So he hurried after her, feeling he might as well see it through.

—How absurd you are, Lavinia, he said, having followed her down two more random turnings. You spend your entire evening searching for me and when we all but fall over one another you make yourself ridiculous by pretending I'm not there.

At which she had to stop.

—I was looking, said Miss Reade, for Sebastian. He is extremely drunk.

—And here he is, said Harrion. For they had reached the bridge.

And, indeed, there was Sebastian standing in a heavy trance swaying at the river. So much liquid and not in a glass seemed to him unnatural.

Now that she was gone he drew a chair to the window and sat looking down on the Marktplatz.

Midnight was striking in sixteen unhurried strokes from the Gemeinehuss. Then from the church the heavy bells crashed with deafening clamour, and to each slow crash the lingering echo that is almost a sob. Ugly and prolonged, the sound swung above the houses like a monstrous noise-scattering censer and under it the pointed unsteady roofs slept a blue sentimental sleep to the fountain's placid rhythm. It ceased; leaving the night to a strained silence which two young priests broke, hurrying past, laughing together.

A moment since she had lit the darkened room like a torch: like a long static flame burning from the floor. Until she spoke. It was her clothes. A something scarlet and over it a straight mannish saffron-coloured dressing-gown suggesting a thing brave and foolhardy: a tongue of fire or the Spanish flag.

But neither her foolhardiness nor her child was of interest to him. From a height he looked down and saw her and was neither interested nor angry nor amused. The anaesthetic of indifference had been administered, it seemed, and under it he had died. So she glowed, she burned about him, announcing her bringing of new birth, yet could not warm him back to life. For he was released from the shell of himself. He who had lived so long among dead things and dead people was now one with them. He too shared their dead life: but knew his deadness. He was not, as they, spines upholding flesh, indifferent to all but their surrounding and immediate needs. An indifference of the will; a coldness of the mind. In detachment absolute he looked about him and knew himself dead among the dead. They, the other dead, believed themselves alive. They found in the movement of an arm or leg a proof of life. But he knew otherwise. Never again was he to need the wine of love or comradeship to make life palatable. But knew that only illness or sudden death could alter that which he was now; and that then this husk-like self would cease to be.

Once he, too, had believed in an after-life, and sightless in the night, in the inky hole of nothingness which is our glimpse into the grave, had leaned on his elbow crying: and shall one never rest? Is there no rest for me? Once tears had poured down his cheeks, he had felt so weak and abandoned to his fear that there might be an after-life.

Suppose one does not die? Suppose there is another life? Suppose they disturb one still and make one's spirit do idle and unprofitable things? Or make one's bloodless body spin through space? (O how d'you do, Mrs Odle-Heming? You spinning through space also? How pleasant is it not, spinning thus through other lives, for ever better, for ever higher?)

Then release is but a longer hell; then peace can never be; then is Death itself the final mockery: the savage jest of a vicious child.

Then why not fade away? Why not dissolve at last into perpetual astral movement and fade away through the ceiling carrying upward one's little lies and one's little goodnesses and one's tea-cup? A sudden thinning and transparence of the flesh: a slow dissolving and elongation on the air. An exit neat and sanitary and decorous. No funeral, no tears, no box, no decomposition, no flowers.

O so-and-so is gone. Have you heard? He faded away before our eyes. He was sitting there and (my dear, it's incredible!) he simply faded away. Up he went: up, up, up.

—How like Paul, Frances would say in her thin and level voice. Anything, *any*thing to annoy me.

For she would meet even Death correctly. Shod, gloved, and clothed as for a journey: inconvenient but unavoidable.

He smiled. For he was safe; borne away on the cold and fathomless sea of indifference which does not give up its dead.

At sixteen he fell in love with Christina Rossetti. He imagined her dark and silent and remote, dreaming ever above sundials, and tended by handmaidens from her brother's paintings. He walked with her across the Downs from Eastdene to Alfriston. He lay on his back, his arms stretched behind his head, feeling the earth breathe under him like some friendly green-furred beast.

She sat the grass as though it were a cloud. She floated there: strayed from the heavenly groves of Orcagna's *Trionfo,* her gown of blue brocade swirling beyond her feet. She sat with transparent hands folded on her lap, following with heavy eyes the lark's effeminate flight. She said: Paul, this I have written for you alone. And slowly unrolling a magnificent illuminated parchment, began with rich melancholy: *I took my heart in my hand, O my love, O my love.*

He must have fallen asleep and when he woke the sun had a chill evening look. He leapt up and set off at a great pace, jingling his hoard of pennies in his pockets. Usually their sound clothed him in the brightest and heaviest suit in the King's armoury and his iron step rang out on the castle courtyard, but now they sang the urgent song of tea and jam and watercress.

Yet he could never bring himself to read about her life; nor had he ever brought her to reality by learning how she lived and among whom. The sight and sound of her name was to him always Browning's dear dead woman. And when people said that there had been no woman poet and that there never could be, he still would say diffidently: there is Christina Rossetti.

He had said so to Lavinia Reade but Miss Reade had dismissed Christina with an abrupt: I dislike those who turn from man to God.

He was amused, for he had met Miss Reade but yesterday, and sixteen was long ago, and Selina had been dead a number of years, and it must have dawned in some other life that morning on which Frances had stepped from behind a burning-bush of lilac, the basket on her arm alight with daffodils, and his heart being young had seemed to break in several different places at once.

But though young not without promise. Indeed, not without achievement, having recently found God in a book of essays which sold 10,000 copies. Having found God in a blade of grass and in the babbling brook and early dew and in other such gentle manifestations of Nature as would ensure (his publishers noted and asked him to luncheon) its steady sale at each hallowed approach of Christmastide and Lent. And even at prize-giving a young tremulous hand might find itself clasping in tooled morocco, scarlet, inscribed, shining-edged: *The Ever-Winding Path*.

The Reverend Lindsay Cressall (writing from Belden, Hants) had been among his first and most urgent admirers: which explains how he came to be standing in the vicarage garden one morning in April. One of those April mornings so fresh, so green, so undiscovered, that one would not be surprised to find oneself covered in grass or patched with cloud or hung about with sky, so part of it one feels. So ardent, so deathless, so purposeful it seems, to be part of the earth's slow stirring to life.

Frances Cressall, the Vicar's third daughter, chose such a moment to emerge from a hedge of lilac, her gardening basket on her arm, her gardening gloves in one hand, and her gardening scissors in the other, engrossed in household thoughts of the familiarity of the butcher's boy with Rose, who was becoming almost insolent of late and who yesterday had sent the tea-cakes in burnt to a cinder: deliberately, of course; and because Prunella (her elder sister) indulged Rose beyond all limits of good discipline.

That afternoon they bicycled in to Christchurch together and Frances smiling gaily, hurried in and out of shops, and in the Priory they held hands beneath Shelley's monument and sighed, compelled to seriousness by the amount of marble on which the poet lay dying; and deciphered that plain stone slab let in the stone floor undated, as pain takes no heed of hour or season.

SALLY WILLIAMS DIED OF GRIEF

and together laughed at its nursery-rhyme simplicity, and particularly (running out to see if the bicycles were still there) at death and grief.

Finally they decided on South Kensington. One of those neat squares of neat houses; genteel of face; correct, column-upheld doorway; windows two by two and expressionless; and Frances indulged her taste, which was three parts Queen Anne, with something solid-coffered and Jacobean in the hall, and something flowery and Chippendale in the bedrooms. And where he was to learn that the flaming sword of Reason steps in only later and (as in the classic story) too late.

He had thought she would be lavish and beautiful in her giving but she was dull and conventional and ashamed.

Uncleverly dull and conventional and ashamed, for it was noticeable. She repelled him by a dutiful submission more suited to a prayer meeting than a marriage bed. A Let us pray lingered on the air with the ghostly echo of a gabbled psalm and before her restrained submission he felt gross and brutal. But she was dutiful in all things, even in things one accepted as part of married life.

Inevitable that her heart should be graven with her household goods: she who had never known a room that was not shared by a grown or growing sister, nor a book nor a ribbon that was not the property of them all. An autopsy on a wife, Harrion had once thought (the early indiscretion of blades of grass and morning dews having been redeemed by years of editorship of a popular-cum-literary weekly) would reveal a dusting brush, a bright array of polished taps, a clock or two admirably precise: the whole culminating in a heart-shaped box of plain English walnut, or inlaid Sheraton, or a slab cut from the Dutch dresser on which how many housemaids had polished off their youth.

For he had learned also that maternity does not necessarily glorify a woman. Even were it not of itself already an ugly function, how unbeautiful they made it by their reluctant and difficult performance. He had been shocked by the unpleasant and unnatural thing it had seemed, the nursing home in which he had paced the hours away; the smell of ether, the forceps, the sense of death and pain. He did not altogether wonder that she seemed to bear him a grudge ever after: seemed secretly to resent it as an injustice against her.

To her intense dissatisfaction their first child was a girl. Possibly the maternal sense of possession (which sucks back the life it has given: which, whether one has loved or hated it, dominates one's days) is not wholly fulfilled in a girl, who, in the end, escapes the more easily and completely. Her not wanting the child made it the more his. He left her the boy, born two years later, partly knowing that she would allow no sharing and the thought of the unequal fight humiliated him, partly having now no need of it.

Ting-a-ling, ting-a-ling. She danced away in front of him ringing like a little bell. That was always his impression of her, that she rang out her own effortless joy as she danced across rooms and pavements. To him she came with everything. Passionate wilful little thing, after she had set her scene and sobbed herself out. She came, placed both elbows on his knees, looked up in his face. Tell me, father, what is it all knotted up inside my head when I'm wicked?

—She makes these scenes, Frances would say coldly, waiting to restore Selina to her nurse, for you to indulge her a little more. If that is possible.

And he would take Selina in his arms, which was like embracing grass, was like a field of buttercups, was newly turned earth. Her young flesh had the sweet clean smell of freshly cut grass.

Through her that April morning lived again. Those sharp eager facets of his soul which time had ground down and experience dulled, shone from her with the poignant gleam of innocence. The best in him, it seemed, though dead was not to die. Nor must it die in her. Let Frances expend her dusting brush and shining taps and inlaid Sheraton heart on her son. His dreams were strange dreams; his schemes had an odd and bitter flavour. For instance, courage. Of all things in life for her, he asked courage. He wanted her courageous; he wanted her brave, even foolhardy. He wanted her generous. He wanted her to give whole-heartedly of herself, her thoughts, her days. He wanted her to love; to love completely and irrationally. And give herself: when the urge came to her she must give herself, without thought, without regret. And be betrayed. And return to him (for to whom else should she turn?) bearing within her the burden of her love: wiser now and hurt, but with no regrets. And he would take her away, away from the outraged Queen Anne (three parts) and the flowery Sheraton bedrooms and the latest carpet-sweeper. South to lazy days under endless sun and watch the child bud and ripen and the life return to her face. For she must be brave and the life within her must not die but glow the more proudly.

It had never seemed quite real to him that when the end came he was not with her. But the telephone bell does not indicate by an altered ring whether its news be good or ill. Nor can one wing with one's desires, nor can one's body precede the lightning of one's thought. Only Frances doing her best to be brave: we must be glad, dear, there was no pain. The end was immediate. As, earlier, the driver of the lorry had stood stammering: It all comes so sudden-like.

He was left alone with her, with nothing but his thoughts of how impotent a thing this love that cannot bridge the bondage of distance, however short. How defenceless love, how inadequate, that not the width of the world can separate more surely than a street, a wall, another room. How powerless love that unless before one's eyes the beloved object does not exist; may call and one does not hear; dies, and a mile away one will be laughing.

How frail this thing on which his life had hung! His Dormouse dead. Gone the threat of putting her in the tea-pot! And to-morrow being Sunday they were to have gone to the Zoo together to see the hippopotamus, her "sweet solid beast" which she preferred to them all; for she no longer searched as on the first day he had taken her, and back again, back again through every house, past each enclosure, until at last despairing, she had had to whisper: Father, no unicorn?

One is, it seems, but the impression one conveys. Nothing more. Only the impression one gives or one receives. All that she was was her impress; and that impress of her all that now remained. A solemn listening face, a field of buttercups, a sudden cry, a ringing of bells. All things that fade, are not renewed; grow dim, are not replaced; and life once good to live has lost its savour.

And then by accident he learned that on a last sudden sign of life she had opened her eyes and called to him. One of those things one is the better, perhaps, for not knowing. But it was not for that that Frances had kept it from him; and knowing this, she was never again quite real to him. So cold and secret his anger that she never guessed. Sensed a difference but never knew; never knew that in the hour of her treachery she, too, had died; but so completely as to leave no memory.

During the War women detached themselves from crowds, or hurried after him across streets, tight-lipped, purposeful: and his horde of feathers grew. Yet all his jingo leader-writing on the *Daily Flare* was more important to them, he often thought, than the one man he might be in a trench as target. And these human targets would they go so willingly to the slaughter if such as he ceased jingoism and Last Penny and Last Man-ing them? Sometimes he wondered did they believe it? But knew there was not one doubt from the breakfast tables of Berkeley Square to the breakfast tables of Balham. They read; they approved; and wrote thanking him for the hope and courage he renewed daily with the toast and marmalade.

He was much in demand at charity *fêtes* where smiling Duchesses raffled lace-and-taffeta cushions and the latest stage favourite kissed the highest bidder. I will give you a kiss and you shall give your life. The type of bargain (he would think grimly) a woman will always make. For he, too, sat upon the platform. There would be cheers, laughter, a loud smacking kiss, the favourite smiling in the direction of the press photographers, a flash, a sharp smell of magnesium; the favourite, clasping flowers, would sit down, and he would leap to his feet and in forceful and compelling voice say very much what he said each morning in print.

It sometimes happened during his tours of the country that here and there among his audiences a voice would ask a question, a question invariably beginning: And why aren't you? So the War Office put him in uniform, and Frances was no longer shamed and affronted as though the whole thing were an insult to herself. And reflected above her pools of tea no longer said quietly: You see, the War Office finds Paul too valuable. The uniform spoke for itself; and with more dignity.

As individual tragedy the War moved him not at all. The collective and incredible heroism of the men who fought: went out in the full-throated ardour of belief, went out again in good-humoured disillusionment, was a dimension of the human soul which neither words nor tears could reach or compass. But the I have given: I have lost: we are giving: we have lost, he saw for what it was. Saw also the dreary record of one mistake after another repeated with the same bravura, the same self-satisfaction, the same shouts, the same bloodshed, the same pomposity; and with a clear sense of what he was doing continued daily to renew the hope and courage of those who sat secure above their toast and marmalade.

Later he attended several Peace Conferences, and came back to find the editorship of a new popular-cum-literary weekly *Book-o-the-Week* abegging, and against the advice of all to whom he mentioned it, decided to accept the offer.

Book-o-the-Week is one of those entertaining and popular weeklies devoted to literature and the idiosyncrasies of the literati, ancient and modern; through which the mass may digest in more palatable form the crumbs from the tables of the erudite: bringing pleasure to the many and indigestion to the few.

Not that the indigestion of the few need be taken seriously.

They well knew the value of a review in *Book-o-the-Week* as against a review in a purely literary paper such as, shall we say?, *The Rambler*. *The Rambler* whose circulation is sluggish: whose advertising is insufficient: whose remunerative rates are negligible. A few sparse political paragraphs, a few sparse initialled essays, a book review or two: from a friend to a friend. The few choice words, whose elegance cloaks their genteel lack of matter, which have been placed this week in *The Rambler* for the pleasure of seeing one's name in its correct setting, are re-written with more matter, more sense, and an almost indecent abandon for next month's *Book-o-the-Week*. *Book-o-the-Week* whose circulation is abundant, whose resources are inexhaustible; which, though not upon the tables of one's friends, carries one's name to that world at large (unrecognised but yet existing): carries also one's photograph. The spiritual weariness of the high-souled is ever dissipated by the sight of an adequate cheque; and the Editor once more casts his nacreous crumbs.

Harrion made few mistakes. He knew (despite our old-world and almost envious contempt of America) that a vulgar robustiousness is preferable to a stagnant gentility. He made his paper a financial and popular success as ably and impersonally as he had made the War palatable to those who could not do their thinking for themselves, and who accepted his assurance that it was as courageous to sit and wait as to fight, and that a blind or mutilated man is as nothing to a woman's anxious heart.

It is Lavinia Reade who described the poetess Eldra Litwell as: *grandmother of all the angels in a Flemish heaven: yet human enough to have the slightly supercilious air of the ducal nursery governess admitting of no familiarity.* And who wrote of her work: *She follows in the footsteps of Rimbaud and finds each footstep a valley.*

It was Lavinia Reade who brought him the essay on

Tennyson in which in her opening sentence she said much that it had taken Mr Lytton Strachey an entire volume to say: *And on the throne a sulky pumpkin.*

Again it was Lavinia Reade who, on the news of D. H. Lawrence's death, startled the office by putting her head on her desk and weeping long and angrily. And later wrote: *It is all very Upper Reaches of the Thames, and Belgravia, and W. 14; so composed, so joyless, so many. It was not merely that he saw clearly this mass unevolved. It was that, seeing clearly, he gave the impression of not being a gentleman. Recognition came at last with his least serious work: The Woman Who Rode Away. That the Woman Rode Away, one feels, had much to do with it. Had she merely walked away genteel curiosity would not have been aroused.*

There was about her work a certain rational madness more sure than any sanity. Which she herself would explain by: I never fish in teacups.

Yet it was exactly at such a party, one of those interminable literary parties at which these island tea-cup fishers sit boasting their catch or belittling the catch of others, that he had met her. Not that she herself was boasting or belittling. She was sitting alone in another room near the bookshelves hurrying through a large and latest *de luxe* edition, and as he came near she looked up and smiled and said: I've saved five guineas. I've been coveting this for weeks, and it isn't worth it!

He sat down. Perhaps he was glad to escape the raised and interpolating voices, the clatter of cups, the overcrowded discomfort, the sense of being a marked man among them. From far the whispered comment, and the approach, the quite unclever approach, of the bored and the serious, the lisping and the soulful, mentioning casual triumphs, inviting themselves to the office when no invitation was forthcoming: until he felt he must be wearing top-boots and an enormous buttonhole, must be cracking an invisible whip, so neatly did the tame ponies prance through their mental paces and through their literary hoops.

Perhaps he liked the wide and eager smile with which she had greeted him; the scarlet frock: a frock a child would choose for best; the neat way her eye took in a page and turned to the next. And not once did she pose for him: neither aware of her legs, nor her nose, nor her hair, nor her hands. She read on, intent and unselfconscious. So he sat and waited and watched her.

As she closed the book and saw him still sitting there, looking at her, she laughed and said:

—If they *will* fish in tea-cups for thirty years what *can* they produce?

He was about to say, but she anticipated him and said quickly: No. I am here only to watch the fishing. I'm a journalist.

So they talked about journalism, which he gathered she detested. But was positively indignant when he said that on principle he disbelieved in all women journalists as they never got the news.

—Tell me, said Lavinia Reade. Do you know anyone who could have got that story out of Samson except Delilah?

So he asked her to come and see him at his office and she came bringing the absurd and irreverent essay on Tennyson. He said (it was a foregone conclusion) I cannot publish this, but. And then asked her to luncheon to talk it over.

It would be untrue to say of Lavinia Reade that she talked. It seemed she smiled and that the words which followed that smile were the articulate expression of its radiance. One felt visibly her abundant life and the bold rhythm of her blood. In her movements, in her words, in that long independent neck, in her silence, one felt the bold rhythm of her heart-beats. It was not merely her youth. Youth (as the advertisements insist) is but a matter of arteries. Youth is ungainly, brave with the bravado of ignorance and to the onlooker peculiarly dull. It was not merely her youth, for on a word, on a silence, she could seem all at once immeasurably old and versed in sorrow, and seeming to have wept through many lives as deeply as she laughed through this one. But unaware of it herself she gave an instant impression of courage, even of foolhardiness; and the bold rhythm of her blood was infectious.

There were more luncheons, and a few book reviews, and finally the offer of a staff job at a salary which made Miss Reade feel that life could play one enchanting tricks and that her uncertainties were over for a little while at least.

Her immediate impression was too unserious not to be resented in the office. A newcomer must be humble. A newcomer must not do with ease that which it has taken others long years of practice to achieve. Wisely other members of the staff, older, experienced, longer in service, resented Miss Reade's unconscious possession of every place she entered. So a few of them put their heads together and showed by their manner exactly what they thought of it all. But they were anticipating by several weeks. Lavinia Reade did not live with Harrion until at least two months after their first meeting. Even though he several times had been down to the flat in Chelsea overlooking the river, bringing with him books, and fruit, and gramophone records. Only to depart leaving Miss Reade staring at the gulls swaying above the water, and wondering why the human heart grows sad because a bird flies past a window and shows silver under the wing.

Possibly it would have continued being a matter of books and gramophone records but for the letter which came one day as she was giving him tea, and Miss Reade, thinking he knew all the gossip about M'Hugh, and Rollo the portrait-painter, and that great white slug of a creature Trinkovitch, the violinist, decided she might as well be hung for a sheep as a lamb, or simply didn't think at all, and looking at the snapshot cried: goodness, how large he's getting! And there in the long-grass of a Cornish field, a round little boy of about three, peeped from behind the heavy skirts of a great sturdy female grinning into the camera. There was not much to see of the little boy for a bunch of hair hung in one eye and the farmer's wife was so very large, but Miss Reade after looking at the picture intently, said: O bother. He's getting as dark and hairy as his father.

Harrion had stared with peculiar satisfaction at the picture. It excited him strangely that she had had lovers and this illegitimate child and that she sent money each week to this massive grinning female, and that with it all she was gay and untouched as a virgin, with a proudly set head and the strong bold rhythm of her heart-beats, which now seemed to him so urgent in their invitation. He sat there staring, staring in a heavy stupor of exultation, and at last heard himself saying something charming about the child. They laughed together; Miss Reade with a peculiar high gaiety, a rush of sound, an eager jet of escaping fear, knowing that the worst was over and she was safe, and would not stand, that afternoon, watching the indifferent gulls swaying above the river, which the barges ploughed with such stubborn energy.

She could see no sense in leaving the office, but he insisted, and she was all obedience. It made it so furtive and she was not used to furtiveness in her love affairs. But he could not bear to see her sitting there before her desk. She must be waiting for him and he must come to her; and as it was the nearest he ever came to a declaration of love she humoured him and found pleasure in her disappointment.

So she sat dutifully and waited, trying not to finger the secret doubts in her mind, and distractedly reading the pages of books two or three times over, and looking up and saying aloud: I love him! I love him! Because it was essential to her to love the men with whom she slept (except of course Trinkovitch to whom she went to show Rollo that one might be discarded but not necessarily despairing, and who *was* a celebrity in his own way, after all, and really more unpleasant in retrospect than in fact).

And because it was so natural to her to love, asking only the opportunity: and each time with abundant zest and as though it were the first time such a thing had happened to her.

But never before had she sat dutifully waiting. And never a word of love. Perhaps it was beyond love this strange thing that had happened to her. It was rather awful the way he came into the room as though expecting her to be ready for him. And hardly an endearment. Afterwards she would lie in that obscene-looking scarlet bed of hers looking at the moon and stars on the absurd blue ceiling, and try not to understand how very different it all was. For it was horrible the way he held her down and consumed her. It was no longer a mutual act, but a thing dark and fearful which he performed despite himself. She thought at first it was because he was a man who had been long denied. But that phase was past and it continued like a war waged against a secret enemy. It seemed a thing he did in fear and secrecy. Some dark forbidden thing, a thing avid, sinful, that he fought to shut out as he held her down, impaled; impaled on the drawn sword between man and woman; enmity eternal. Yet he seemed scarcely conscious of her. He drained her in this dark and secret way. And the result left her lost and impaled, so that she sat and waited for his return; a thing she had never done and could not have conceived herself ever doing. She would look up from the page she had re-read three times and say aloud, with her head thrown back: I love him! and feel warm and satisfied and proud with love, as she understood it. Almost her old self. She needed again this spoken day-lit assurance of normality.

But he would come back and the thing would begin again, like some unspeakable vice, some dance with death. And all day long she had been waiting for it. All day long she sat and waited. And when he did not come she felt leaden and bruised and resentful and loathed herself for what seemed more a morbid habit than love as she had known it.

Now the ebb and flow of her blood was not so swift and careless. Nor was the rhythm of her heart-beats so bold. The bright virginal look was becoming a little pinched and vicious. But he did not notice it, though she looked pale and used-up and rather ethereal, like a bewildered vicious child. She rarely went out. She would sit at the open window and revert to her old fancy of imagining lives for the people who idled beside the river and sat beneath the mottled plane trees. And would think disjointedly: I love him, I love him. Then all at once would feel resentful and held prisoner. She looked awful: awful. And he never noticed it! Like a fool, like a whore she ached and waited and allowed herself to be ploughed beyond her strength. He burnt her up and she stood it no better than Semelle stood it. And never once had he told her he needed her. Nothing for her. Only this rapt consuming fire of his which slowly and relentlessly extinguished hers.

So she sat at the window and waited, wondering was this what it meant: whom the gods love die young. Wondering was this how women waited in turret tops, bent above tapestry frames. But that could not be: for how gay and impudent they were! And only love fulfilled is gay and impudent. And going to the gramophone she put on: Belle Doëtte à sa fenestre se sied. And then: En revenant dedans les champs, Avons trouvé les blés si grands.

And called it education, the spread of gentility. So that no-one now waited in turret tops and was gay and impudent about it. For what heed takes genteel education of reeling and writhing and laughing and grief? It was the shopping-hour and they hurried in their droves, all passionately clutching little paper bags of inexpensive silk stockings. And the needle, too, was for other uses. The needle trilled

> . . . les blés si grands,
> La blanche épine florissante
> Devant Dieu....

and Lavinia Reade trilled with it, for there are words born as a caress to the soul whether it lies (officially) between the eyes or the breasts. La blanche épine florissante devant Dieu! I want a garden, thought Lavinia Reade, fingering the record gently and wondering would tears wash away its song. I want to sit and wait in a garden. Every woman, she thought, looking at the sullen unhurrying river and weeping bitterly, should have a garden in which to sit and wait. So she sat down and began a short story of some-one who wanted a garden in which to sit and wait, and the afternoon was gone unnoticed.

In another such abnegation would have seemed to her unpardonable. She would have protested and been full of theories. But the very strangeness of the experience, the sense of guilt and immolation, the troubled sense of its abnormality, was the measure of its fascination for her. Secretly she was appalled at the resentful satisfaction she felt at sitting and waiting; the sensual ease with which she assumed the role of odalisque. So she stared at the printed page and said I love him! I love him! as though to gloss with charm and familiarity the gross and the unfathomable.

She wrote several short stories; unequal, diffused. She would read them to him knowing them frankly bad, and be shocked by his easy acceptance of each as a minor masterpiece. Indeed, his attitude to her work had changed. Now he indulged her. He was good-natured about it and pleasantly encouraging, as though she were playing with a new and difficult toy by his especial consent.

She had the impression that soon he would correct the pages and add good conduct marks. So she put them away in a drawer, unable to destroy that which had cost her so much useless effort to produce; and to save herself from dying piecemeal of a pernicious mental anæmia (as she put it) insisted that he bring her books to review. But they were uniformly artless and unreal, unflavoured, thoughtless; and she was uniformly irritated and impudent about them, untroubled by qualms of conscience.

She was more troubled about her looks. Troubled also about her mood, which grew increasingly melancholy and resentful. She looked awful and still he did not notice. But Clare Sefton noticed. They ran at one another in the King's Road early one afternoon; Miss Reade under her friend's bold scrutiny carrying languidly the pose of love too well requited. She learned that she was rumoured to be in Italy: but not with whom, for opinion was divided. She learned that Simon Linsey was giving a party at his studio. And that M'Hugh had been asking for her; and that M'Hugh would be there. So she accepted and felt quite gay at parting. She must show M'Hugh her new look of a bewildered vicious child. Tired and languid and remote she would sit, wilting and bored, among the merry-makers; and would wear her most circumspect and spinsterish gown, for never is vice more alluring than when clothed in discretion.

Unfortunately by the evening the excitement of her plan, for which she alternately reproached and applauded herself, had brought the colour to her cheek and her eyes were quick and mischievous. So that Harrion arriving unexpectedly (to find her in a long black satin frock curling short tendrils of hair to a studied rebelliousness) saw her lively eyes and peremptorily asked where she was going, and not unnaturally assumed that the meeting was clandestine and desirable. She told him where she was going; knowing as she spoke that she would not be going yet continuing gravely to aggravate the tendrils of hair. She let him storm and reiterate for fully half an hour before kicking aside her high brocade slippers and pulling off the long tight frock, spoiling the curled masterpiece of a head. Astonished she stood listening to the crude and unreal arguments with which he fought. One would have thought she was about to compromise herself irrevocably. One would have thought it was her first illicit party and that she was caught as she escaped to it. She refused to believe that he was serious. Something about his anger struck her as unpleasant and curiously impersonal. When she had listened long enough to harsh and peremptory commands such as: I forbid you to be seen in such a place, she stopped him by the wintry irony of her voice: Quite. I know my place. Then burst into tears and said that she was tired, and sobbed herself out in his arms; and he was very tender and gentle with her.

He took her to the Zoo, and though she called the zebra a donkey from Rodier (which delighted him), it was not a success. For Miss Reade was more interested in those before the cages. Had her remarks been naïve, but they were harsh; and once in the ape house were so insistent that he had had to hurry her out. But the restless to-and-fro oppressed her. In the end she walked through every house, past each enclosure, speculating on which caged thing was the most unhappy; and stopping at the golden crested eagle, knew unerringly.

With polar bears cavorting in the background they sipped tea in the sparse sunshine, and Miss Reade developed her theory of how did one wish to convert animals to religion, one would find one's converts only in the Zoological Gardens of the world. But do not open the cages, even after they are convinced and baptised. One could never be too sure with the eagle, for instance.

The following Sunday he took her to Kew Gardens. Willows hung in thin green ropes above the varnished lake. Small yellow ducks threw in their heads and became crocuses. A blackbird put forward his most shining notes. She felt again the beating of the grassy pulse. The beautiful sane green enveloped her.

She ran full tilt over the grass between the trees; then stood waiting for him to come up to her. Another, she could not help feeling, would have run with her, sharing equally the immediate release of gaiety which the sudden sight of trees and grass must always bring the town dweller. But that, she thought, watching him staid and smiling in the distance, was the symbol of their relationship; the waiting was hers. Though knowing the moment too keen and brief to dissipate in words, she tried to be gay and light-hearted to please him. And all at once walking beside him, her hand in his, it occurred to her that this was not herself at all, but was one of Madame Tellier's young females out walking with a kind-hearted habitué. The cruel aptness of the thought shocked her to laughter; and he asked the reason, glad to see her carefree and happy.

Miss Reade replied with a bright immediacy (infallible sign that a woman is lying): I was thinking that what one most admires in D. H. Lawrence is his sturdy independence. He called a table-napkin a serviette to the end.

But he did not seem to relish her wit as he used to. Yet it was keen as ever; so keen that she would not go again to Kew. So, having no garden, she resigned herself to waiting beneath her absurd starry ceiling; staring at the Thames and wishing it were the Seine; discovering that the baubled plane tree is (surely) the invention of a child; and wondering whether her suspicions of the last few days were justified. Not that she cared. In such things her mind was simple and uncomplicated. It was neither a matter for heroics nor repugnance. However, she kept her suspicions to herself for it was too soon to be certain; and even when certain, hesitated. For she clung to the new dark harmony of her life; and at the thought of losing him her resentment left her.

For none knew better that what is desirable in a wife is unpardonable in a mistress. Men were such irrational and frightened creatures. Their sense of honour, or the sense of morality, or sense of responsibility, was always being affronted and made to bear burdens too large for it. The spinster with child was indefinably incorrect. Strange how a man could never feel himself the proud father of his mistress's child! Paternal joy, it seemed, was primarily a legal matter; and in all other cases was a cause either for annoyance, for downright anger, or for a tender pity. It was the tender pity that Miss Reade feared most. It occurred to her that Eve must have borne her punishment cheerily enough and not until she surprised the first look of tender pity on Adam's face did she curse the serpent in her heart. At least M'Hugh had been furious; though later recovering his good humour they went out and celebrated the occasion with unaccustomed ceremony; yet though they were together almost a year after the child was born, she knew exactly in which moment she had lost him.

Although she chose the moment wisely and her words with care, she could not she told herself have foreseen the effect it was to have on him. Afterwards it even occurred to her that had one been suggesting a suicide pact he could not have shrunk from her more palpably. When at last he had left with nothing but that incoherent stammer which she could not catch, she lay down in dismay with her face in the pillows. The next day passed in hope and despondency, and the next and the next. After the third day of sitting by the telephone in a torpor from which she roused herself only at the postman's knock, she rang up the office, to be told that he was away and they did not know when he would return. Then she knew that it was no use sitting and waiting. She was so utterly and incredibly alone that there seemed no place for her to go, so she went to bed; now and then shaken from her thoughts by the undaunted Emily standing with a tray and saying: now, now, Miss, there's nothink like a cupertea I always ses. Have you ever been in love, Emily? asked Miss Reade, aware of Emily's large and placid charm; and Emily holding the tea-cup and bending over her with large maternal impatience, thought: p'raps I seen enough of it with you, me paw dear.

After a fortnight his cheerless impersonal letter arrived with a foreign postmark, assuring her of unfailing financial aid.

—But it would never *occur* to me to worry over money! cried Miss Reade to the letter she was holding, unable to understand the argument that money is the unfailing substitute.

It had not occurred to Harrion that to Miss Reade the essential thing in the letter was his address; possibly because Lavinia Reade as a reality no longer existed for him. Nor ever had. The moment she had told him about her child, bringing their relationship as it were to life, he knew exactly what he had done. He knew what he had always known: that he was a man ridden by the ghost of what could never be.

A moment since and she had called him ill. He was not ill. To be ill is to feel pain, to know sensation, to desire to be well. He was not ill. He was beyond illness. Nor was his mind affected. Only the anaesthetic of indifference had been administered and under it he had died.

Once more bells disturbed the night, maliciously accenting the half-hour as though there must be no sleep for the faithful. It occurred to him suddenly that Christ did not live long enough. After the perfect love would have come the perfect indifference.

The whole earth sang in circles round the sun! Rounded hills, rounded clouds, rounded tree-tops, and wave upon wave of incoming hill. A concourse of meadow-swifts wrote a Gregorian chant on the telegraph wires. Drawing an empty cart, two pale unhurried oxen with vacant mummer's masks came over the cobbles with the abstracted stare of the sleepwalker. A busy dog was at his nasal observations. A white horse, round and clean as a goose, was being led to the fountain to drink.

Tossing a comb through her hair and tossing her head, Miss Reade was at her window, well-pleased with the view. She put from her mind all night-thoughts of Italy. Besides she had just seen Harrion walk across the little square and vanish down a side turning. Elbows on sill she had watched him walk away from her. O the completeness of the male who by the mere act of walking away can stress his arrogant isolation! No woman can walk away so completely dead to all things around her. Her hips flutter; her legs look ridiculous and inconclusive, the whole of her is aware of being watched, and irritated by this inescapable awareness of others. Women were scattered in body and scattered in mind; somatic; ever-alert. But the very physical compactness of a man stressed his isolation. So that by chance, looking at a given moment from a window, one surprised this male aura of unapproachableness and indifference. Well, there he went and with him Italy!

Now the incredibly clean horse had finished his drink and was moving off at a merry trot. Two small boys with satchels flying at their backs, chased each other around the fountain. Miss Reade removed her comb and herself to the mirror, reflecting that because the sunlight had played on her face as she watched, a significant thing had seemed almost impersonal; for which, had it happened at night, she would have tossed and re-tossed, accepted and refused, and wearied the hours with whys and nevers. Yet there he was walking away from her in the early sunshine and her thoughts were full of hot coffee. It must be that one dies at night; one dies the small death of sleep and one's vitality is low. The scale of light falls on the mood as on the day. She must remember that.

In the Wynstub Lorwich and Sebastian Doyle were discussing Protection and Mr Ramsay MacDonald. It must have been Mr Ramsay MacDonald for she caught frequent allusions to

Little Orphan Annie and Salvation Jane. Lorwich had finished his coffee and was talking across a newspaper. Sebastian sat before his usual breakfast of Traminer and small brezeln. From afar he rose and greeted Miss Reade with elaborate courtesy. Lorwich ignored her. He was saying: So now your London manufacturer brings me my turban or my loin cloth and asks me ten shillings. I see the rest of the world buying that yard of cloth for one shilling. Therefore the British Government is levying on me an extravagant and unbearable tax of every indispensable article I buy; therefore Protection means being ordered to buy the most expensive goods and not necessarily the best: the tea-tax lost America: this would not merely lose India but cause a revolt in every corner of the Empire; who to-day will stand the injustice of being made to pay more for not-always the best goods?; and in many cases having to accept substitutes for the genuine article because England does not happen to produce it? Enforce the exchange of Empire trade and the result will be more swift and disastrous than the enemies of England can wish. (Sebastian nodded and drained his glass.) Besides, in modern goods Britain was behind the times; no-one wanted tin spoons to-day; they wanted Woolworth silvered nickel; novelty and change required elasticity of mind and adaptability: hardly the forte of our British manufacturer, who leaves the nonsense of producing what the world really wants to France, to Germany, to America, to Czecho-Slovakia.

(Käthe, some coffee! Und noch ein viertel, shouted Sebastian.) The British industrialist has proved himself incapable of competing with the rest of the world. Why? Because we British bring our damned caste superciliousness even into trade: anything is good enough for the other fellah. Even in sport we have sought a spurious mental Protection. We have coined the formula that we are gentlemen and the rest of the world professionals, and that we take graciously as diversion what the rest of the world takes as hard work. And there's your whole difference between England and the rest of the earth. A few gentlemen taking things lightly: and highly trained specialists taking them seriously.

Käthe who had been telling Miss Reade that it made one happy to see the sun again after so much rain, flounced away to attend to Lorwich. Käthe always flounced when attending to Lorwich. Her sense of fitness was revolted. Here, indeed, was a good man wasted.

Miss Reade helping herself to the glassy dark-green mountain honey which the bees had gathered in the pine woods, reflected not without malice that no much-married City man could be more aggressive at the breakfast table on certain mornings than could Lorwich. And not even a train to catch. Could it be that he was throwing at politics and the amiable Sebastian the Jovian bolts he had not dared hurl at Corydon?

For Simeon Fenn was not to be seen at so earth-bound a meal as breakfast. Not thus did he reveal himself to mortals. But springing pale and ineffable upon the world (possibly an hour hence) the fair-tressed Apollo, cloud-throned, would appear in the Wynstub doorway and with eyes for none but Lorwich, would utter languidly: I am going for a walk.

Going? It could not be going? Gliding. Or leaping. Or wafting. But going?

Meanwhile Lorwich having turned to the next item on his newspaper was saying that though less benefit to the Bankers than they had hoped, nothing did us so much good as beating Germany. It had got Germany down to work, scientifically advancing the world twenty-five years, while we sit and watch her do it and wonder how it's done. Thanks to the Allies Germany has no military service: consequently Germany has a million picked young brains from whom to choose to do her work. She has no fortifications, no armaments, and therefore more leisure for progressive thought.

So Germany builds; and England stagnates; and France has an army of a million young men to keep in idleness, and nothing to show for Peace but hundreds of little blue soldiers leaning over bridges.

Sebastian nodded and re-filled his glass. Breakfast was not his hour for argument. Also he had been extremely drunk the night before.

From where she sat Miss Reade could see in profile the motion as he talked of Lorwich's rusty beard. And to think that that man had a wife and children perennially suing for maintenance in the English courts while he, on and off, was being politely asked to leave most of the countries he entered.

Squat and gross and powerful, he carried well his deliberate unwashed and unkempt audacity. He had (Miss Reade decided) a subtle and rather pleasing beauty of dirt: that careless beauty of dirt such as one surprises in the true peasant, or in those Italian road workers who grin mischievously up at one as the train passes. Definitely one could admire his robust unkemptness as against such purely negative elegance of well-washed flesh as Simeon Fenn. Which arrogant sense of dirt Lorwich carried also into his work; for (when the Coterie glamour of his personality was discounted, reflected Miss Reade) what were his works but a few salacious post-cards taken haphazard from his literary pocket and distributed in signed copies at so many guineas apiece? But it paid: the glamour, and the dirt, and the Coterie. And particularly the elegant Fenn.

Ach, said Käthe, returning to Miss Reade's corner and leaning from the open window. Ach, it made one happy to see the sun again after so much rain. Ach, could it but last!

A group of holidaying Germans with heavy rucksacks strapped, and large bare knees, marched across the little square singing one of their honest good-natured songs in which the best of friends are for ever parting.

And Lavinia Reade sighed as she sipped her coffee. There he had slunk away, who knew where?, when one should be walking (like this) bare-headed and singing in the morning sunshine. What had she achieved in a week of being here? Twice by waylaying him she had been for a short walk, mostly in silence, for he had nothing to say but that she was provided for and need have no worry. Well and what had she expected? To bring him to her knees again? A line from a poem she had been reading in a literary review came back to her: Iniquitous, knee to knee. No. There seemed no possibility of bringing him to her knees. Then, to her feet? But he never had been at her feet and he no longer wanted her at his. But he is ill, she reflected, he is ill. But how cold, how dead he was in the sudden unapproachable indifference which he seemed to have spun about him in an aura of decay. And what he was trying to do (O she knew) what he was trying to do was to get away again, to escape her as soon as the best scheme presented itself; and this time leave no address.

—Ach, sighed Käthe drawing-in her head, it made one happy to see the sun again after so much rain.

And there was Lorwich still talking. The room droned with the rumblings from his rusty beard. He seemed to be re-writing in argument the entire newspaper. He had now reached the Come to Britain movement. And of all the damned silly nonsense, when the only salvation for England lay in shutting her doors and keeping to herself, instead of inviting inspection. When only the milords came out of England—the others remaining in a dense fog—the world supposed the rest equal to the sample. But, behold, modern communication and the cinema and the radio had dispersed that fog and revealed the ass under the British lion's skin.

And then poised and languid in the doorway, Simeon Fenn was saying: I am going for a walk; and Lorwich was on his feet, crumpling his newspaper under one arm and stumping across the room in unseemly haste; and Miss Reade was staring rather deliberately toward the window, for though not liking the man she knew his worth, and did not care to see him playing Hercules in petticoats to this lisping inferior; and even Sebastian, who took tactless delight in all things, was studying a brezel as though it were the contortion of a playful grass snake.

But soon he must cross to Miss Reade's table and looking down at her, say: I am going for a walk.

She refused to smile and instead said petulantly: why must you drink wine in the early hours of the morning?

—Possibly to endure more equably the Lover at the Breakfast Table. Why must you drink coffee?

Miss Reade having lost the round, went and got her walking stick, for though Sebastian might be irritating in argument he took the hills with a cloven hoof.

And there, down a side-turning as they all but reached the Andlau Tor, they saw it, small and round and serious, standing on a pile of sand and holding up a little wooden spade and bucket. The infant, surprised by their shouts of recognition, lifted a fat sulky face and stared.

There was no mistake. It was he! And this the first time they had seen him on land. Usually he sat behind the bin in the little manure cart which his brothers, purposeful with their shovels, drew out of the gates each morning on to the main roads. Wherever one saw the little cart, at standstill by the roadside as the children munched their food, or being pulled home at night, there he sat round and solemn and sulky behind the small bin, now full with the day's good gathering. And the very first time they had seen him, such a miniature comedian, such a baby clown, with his high-domed head, his querulous curving brows, the look that he might cry if spoken to, his pugnacious nose and humorous mouth, so serious, so amiable, so delightfully softly incompetent, with everything there but the funny bow and eccentric hat, they had stood still in the street and shouted as one man: *Winston!* And here he was, fat and serious on the top of a sand heap, looking as though about to harangue his bucket.

Startled by their shouts of welcome, and with the suddenness of all well-calculated drama, Winston overbalances and becomes a girl.

—O! cried Lavinia Reade too affronted to help him up. O. O. Now I don't know *what* to call you, for there is nothing in the female line quite so pompous as Winston Churchill....

—Come, come, said Sebastian, astonished. There is — —, and — — —, and — —.

They argued it all the way to Blienschwiller.

But it was not to take the hills with Sebastian that she was here. Nor to assault woods, full with wildboar and gazelle and mosquito, that she had abandoned her bed under its starry ceiling.

And Sebastian was talking; talking in his amiable unhurried voice, that droned among her stubborn thoughts till she took heart and abandoned them. For Sebastian was telling the story of his friend Basil Ollan; and it seemed right that as he told it they should turn from the plain over which the small dark trees were dotted in a pox, and walk on and upward, straight into a sky outstretched like a summer's sea beneath a small thin white sand of fleecy cloud, in which a faint shell of moon still drifted.

Every-one knows the story of Basil Ollan inasmuch as one knows that he committed suicide in a rather grim and delightful manner: choosing the dining-room to do it in, seated ironically at the head of the table, and serving himself up to them for breakfast, as it were, with a slit throat and a bloodstained razor.

They said that he did it as an advertisement for his book *Self-Portrait in a Coffee Pot* which had appeared a month earlier. A shallow deduction, since the *Self-Portrait* was the literary success of years and needed no further effort from his part. Or they said that he did it to spite his excellent spouse and deprive her of the only lion she had not been able to appreciate.

For every-one knows the story of Mrs Basil Ollan; that inveterate and courageous hunter of literary lions, to whom the London artistic jungle is one long safari; aided and abetted by one son, an exquisite performer on the clarinet and the virginals, and those twin daughters, who dress alike, who smile alike, and are given to toe-dancing in their mother's drawing-room at day and evening parties with practically nothing on.

The lions laugh; but do not stay away. Living retired, domesticated, and uneventful lives, they realise the importance of such women as Mrs Ollan, who woo and entice them, and show them to advantage against silvered walls, among the lilies and the cocktail bars and the salted almonds and the journalists. The lions laughed a good deal when it was found that the insignificant little man with pale unseeing eyes who would sometimes be noticed sitting in a corner staring in his cocktail glass as though it were poisoned, and whose conversational brilliance began and ended with Quite. Quite. I agree. Could roar of his own accord, and louder and longer than any of them (it is feared) in his *Self-Portrait in a Coffee Pot*. Mrs Ollan laughed also; for the one way to parry ridicule is to gather it up and rejoice in it, and make full and laughing confession.

She staged an immense party for the *Self-Portrait*. The toe-dancing twins learned some of the more ribald contortions of negresses at their intestinal exercises. The Boy sat at his spinet with limpid profile averted. Basil Ollan instead of being somewhere in a corner was standing as though nailed in the very centre of the room. And three days later seated ironically at the head of the dining-room table he sent the underhousemaid into a screaming fit that lasted throughout the morning.

Mrs Ollan's large circle of friends agreed that the poor man had no alternative with such a woman; her enemies on the whole were rather sorry for her. His publishers were naturally delighted, for a dead author is more valuable than a live lion; whilst it was charitably accepted by the Coroner that the nervous strain of a successful book had been too much for the victim. And all the time Basil Ollan had done merely what he had intended doing years ago, but had been too preoccupied, until recently, to set about.

His will held no malice. The Twins and the Boy and their Mother were not humiliated publicly, nor made to feel, beyond the doubts in the minds of their friends, that the dining-room comedy was staged on their behalf. There was, however, a point which long puzzled Mrs Ollan. A cheque for two thousand pounds in her husband's name had been withdrawn from the bank about a week before his suicide, and the money could not be accounted for and certainly had not been spent. But she who had no discretion, was for once discreet. The publicity had been enough.

Meanwhile the money was in Sebastian's pocket. For Sebastian knew of the suicide long before it happened; years before it happened: and also one week before it happened. He even knew of the *Self-Portrait* as it was being written, and had helped with the proof-reading. But at that time Sebastian was not asked to Mrs Ollan's whip-cracking parties; except by proxy when all unknowing she once entertained the highly successful author of the highly successful review, much of whose songs and sketches had been written by the amiable Sebastian.

On the day he withdrew the money from the Bank Ollan had arrived at his friend's rooms in Clifford's Inn with a suitcase packed with papers (with which Sebastian must do as he chose) and the tobacco jar he had used for nearly thirty years, and an array of obviously valuable dress-studs for which he apologised nervously, and putting these down he began to talk of the two thousand pounds which he handed over in an envelope. He was brief, for he was not a talkative man (which silences, incidentally, are among the solaces of the friendships of men). He gave Sebastian an address and vague directions as to how one got there; accepted a brandy and soda; sat smoking awhile, and was gone without even a handshake. And it was not until a few hours later when Sebastian chose to wonder why in the name of God a heap of papers and magnificent dress-studs should be planted on him, as it were, without explanation, that he realised what was going to happen. But he loved the man too much to go to him and remonstrate.

About a week after the news was in the evening papers Sebastian remembered his errand and proceeded to drive himself to Cornwall. Ordinarily it was not a pleasure he would have undertaken willingly. For Sebastian was one of those on whose heart Calais is engraved, and who, when they think of Spring or beauty, turn their heart's eye to other lands. To him the English countryside was but so much unchanging mile of hedgerow, servility, and bad beer. However, Cornwall is the least restrained and gentlemanly of all the slices into which this island is divided against itself. It is stubbled and bleak and thrust out into a cold sea, into an ugly mass of tin shack and towering rock called Land's End. And arrived there he turned to the right and drove for miles across moors, and through stony hovelled villages lost in what seemed a land of famine, and once again on to a moor, till he came to that wan lurching house set alone in a sea of stone and heather.

So it was here that Ollan had housed his mistress and kept his long secret even from his friend.

It was not a pleasant task that he was about to do, and in this abandoned setting Ollan's death was very near to him. As he stopped the car and got out, his hands were trembling. So he stood awhile to steady himself and stared at the ghostly house, and at the sea of stone and heather, and at the evening sky. A milky sky: one of those evening skies so pale that there is no-thing there. One looks up and there is no-thing there.

Yet the garden, once he had lifted the latch, was full of blue and velvety colour and a warm earthy smell. But there seemed no one about. What a fool's errand! He knocked and knocked; and at last went round to the back of the house and peered through a window. And saw there, in a kitchen and with her back to him, a woman knitting in a rocking-chair. So he knocked on the window, and after a surprisingly long time she turned her head and saw him.

When she came to the door he said: Good evening. Does Mrs Maria Ebbisham live here?

The woman stared at him. A red-faced woman with heavy eyes and big upstanding breasts; her two hands in the pockets of a large blue apron.

He repeated the question and this time she shook her head and pointed to her ear. To try again he shouted the question, and now she smiled and again shook her head and pointed to her mouth, and then to her ear and mouth and back again, so that he should understand that she was deaf and dumb. So he took out the envelope on which her name and address were written and showed it to her. But again she smiled and shook her head. She could not read. She was deaf and she was dumb and she could not read.

And that was altogether too much for Sebastian. He began to laugh and went on laughing. He leaned against the doorpost and laughed and roared and rocked with laughter, till his sides ached and his throat was sore.

But it was she. She led him to Ollan's room, where he was to spend the night. A white-washed room bound and held together by black curving beams; a room so old that it seemed to heave and sway and right itself again; a room that can but close about one and give one up, and on which one leaves no impress. The bed was enormous under a brightly stitched counterpane. Beside a window a table piled with books and papers; a fountain-pen with ink dried on the nib, two much-used pipes, and a tobacco pouch. Small used things which one should take with one in the grave (Sebastian thought) for thus abandoned they are more unreal than the dead.

Now the sky had asserted itself and darkened and brought forth one bold green star; and the silence was so palpable that it was right that all born under it in this waste of heather and sky, should be born speechless and without sound.

Lying in Ollan's bed he was awake a long time thinking of the woman with her deep upstanding breasts and large unhurried movements and her silence, and of the peace she must have brought him. By god, what a solid and fathomless rock on which to build one's church! And here, in this room, he had written the *Self-Portrait*. And what a cook! He would have given much to know whether she now spent her night in tears or in sleep. Not in tears. No, not in tears. She would leave weeping to the official widow. She slept. One knew that she slept her steady untroubled sleep. Besides, to-morrow was Monday. And on Mondays one must be up before six. For Monday (everywhere) is always a washing day.

We shall be late, said Lavinia Reade, as turning a corner they saw at last the long black crooked steeple struck like an Inquisitor's bonnet above the houses. We shall be late and Madame will be cross again. But we can do it—if we run.

As a warrior's recreation Madame Jonat was not a success. Although at the moment decked in her silks and finery and spread as invitingly as a nuptial bed, in such capacity she was not at her best. A frigid woman, who took out such energy in hard rages and ugly palpitating fits of temper, violence, and recrimination. Who seemed for ever oppressed by the strain of keeping her head above fat that circled and submerged her: the last waves of which broke against her chin. A heavy white moon of a woman without light or warmth of her own.

Even stretched (as now) in her festal satins Madame's essential self was not more affable. Indeed, was noticeably less so; for the sheen though of silk had the malevolence of armour. But that the intention was festive could be seen in Madame's shrill pomeranian, the rat-eyed Clo-Clo, who wore on his neck his Sunday bow, and was fluffed and arrogant as a pouter pigeon. And by Nicole, Madame's seven year old, that sallow irritable wisp of bone and temper, who seemed more the outcome of her mother's spirit than of her flesh. Nicole who also wore satin, of an uncompromising blue and very short, and among whose black curls flew a bunch of tufted silk.

Seated behind the bar on the raised curved horsehair sofa so oddly like herself, Madame stared at the Wynstub ceiling: that gracious undulating ceiling with richly carved beams, from which the special cast had been taken when, with more good-will than taste, in spacious pre-war days the Germans had restored the Hoch Königsberg and made of it a museum of Alsatian domestic architecture.

Madame was not thinking of the ceiling's undulating grace. She was thinking that cette Mees Ridd and the Monsieur Sebastian were late again; and that not once during the entire week had she known either of them punctual at a meal. A party of strangers was in a far corner of the room; but none of Madame's foreign guests had turned up to luncheon. The Monsieur Leriche and his friend she did not expect. Nor ce pauvre Monsieur (quand même un drôle de type) who had, as usual, dispâru. But cette Mees Ridd and the Monsieur Sebastian: it was too much. Evidently it was not for the English, that cursed and misshapen race, whose palate was dulled with swallowing fog and cokketelle, that one hung one's culinary diplomas about the walls. A race that buys its *soupe* in little cubes and its meat in ice, regards constipation as a national virtue and wine as wicked, and chemist shops as God's greatest gift to man. A barbarous race that should have its food mixed in bowls and served it on the floor!

But to-day no more. After two o'clock nothing for the Mees Ridd. Ab-so-lu-ment no-thing. Karl, cried Madame, après deux heures on ne mange plus rien; deux heures juste, vous entendez. And Karl told Käthe, and winked.

So that it was prophetic and fortunate that Miss Reade had told Sebastian they must run, for when at last they arrived hot and panting in the Wynstub there were a good thirty minutes to spare; and Käthe was delighted. Sweet soul, she hopped about, live as a bird, bringing everything that was wanted before it could be asked.

Miss Reade arching her long independent neck, knew that Madame was displeased again; despite the smile, despite the polite inclination of the head. But why was she all-dressed-up? Miss Reade longed to ask but nothing could have made her: for Madame longed to tell, and would tell just as soon as the moment offered itself. It was not Sunday. Was there a wedding?

Miss Reade smiled gaily at Nicole who, feeling very fine to-day, squirmed in the doorway for all to see. And thought again: what a dreary parody of childhood! And what a largesse of maternal flesh. And how vaguely indecent women were with their fleshy charms hung about them like trophies. Nature has its humours, but it could not be that such an acreage of bosom had been grown to wean this undersized apology of a child? And, decidedly, it was not for the dalliance of her husband: of that one could be certain. Even were its aspects less forbidding, Otto preferred his cellar: and who could blame him?

Indeed, who could blame Otto for anything? mused Lavinia Reade, who adored the masculine virtues. And Otto had them all. Solid, squarely planted, stubborn, cool-tempered, friendly, impersonal. His day's work done he put it from him and gathered his friends for talk and wine, and cards as an excuse for more wine. And the rounder and redder Otto grew and the more full and warm his voice, the more Madame, perched behind the bar, twisted her lips and was affectedly amiable. Madame (did you offer it) graciously drank with you as a particular concession, though more, one suspected, "for the house" than for herself But Otto drank with any one. Any one, that is, whose eye was humorous and whose face was friendly. Otto could go out on the Marktplatz and bring in any thing from beggars to priests and stuff them with food and drink for the pleasure of hearing them laugh. And made one feel how right it was, drinking and being drunk, and leaving one's friends to sleep it off over (or under) one's table in open acknowledgment of one's hospitality.

Lorwich adored him; and in the evening he could ignore Simeon Fenn (very pink and restrained and looking-on) for hours while he out-drank and out-shouted Otto. And from far Madame watched, looking everywhere but at her husband. Taking in the scene on the very first evening Lavinia Reade (who had a quick eye for the human comedy) had thought how like it was to altar panels of Heaven and Hell, with for centre-piece the wine and Sexual Triad, and on the Right Hand the robust and the joyful and on the Left the soured and the ungainly. And thought how, if Otto was very much a man, Madame was all-woman; with a woman's addiction to small pleasures and tantrums, and futilities, and no silence.

But what one could not forgive her, thought Lavinia Reade (stirring her coffee and smiling again at some facial pleasantry of Nicole), what one could not forgive was this anæmic sore-eyed child, when Otto should have sons like himself; strong, easy-tempered male creatures, to work as he worked.

The long table near the door had filled, and Madame as she drew the beer, raised her voice. No, she would take the auto-bus. No. It would arrive in Sélestat in plenty of time. It was an inconvenience. But it was just. It was just that she should tell what she had heard. It was an inconvenience. But it was just.

—The girl is mad, said the man with the neat black beard.

Madame pursed her lips: That we do not know.

—The old woman should be guillotined, said a young peasant with a pink square face. And before she knew it, Lavinia Reade had called Hear! Hear! and tossed her head, and thought how right youth always is.

So it was to attend the trial of the Mère Hunon that Madame was in her festal silks and the dog and child wore satin bows.

—But the girl is mad, shrugged the man with the neat black beard. You'll see. The old woman will get off.

Whereupon Nicole rushed to the middle of the room and shrieked in her high falsetto: I'd kill her. I'd kill them all. I'd kill the Judge, too. And then I'd kill everyone here. Everyone. But not you, she said turning nicely to Lavinia Reade. I'd make one of the men kill you first.

—Loathly little beast, thought Miss Reade, joining gaily in the general merriment.

And then one of the men started laughing at the picture of Monsieur le Curé who had come on the mad girl in a ditch with nothing on but a torn rag of chemise. A winter's night a year ago, she had managed to escape at last and lay shivering in a ditch. And the priest had found her there, jabbering away, in her filthy rag of a shirt, a body covered with sores and wounds, and blood still trickling from her head and from her mouth where most of the teeth had been knocked out. And the priest, with gentle words and with infinite patience, had soothed the inhuman creature, and had led her back; had led her back to the mother who had kept her tied in a dark shed for years and starved and tortured her. And the priest had never mentioned the meeting. *Madame Hunon est si dévôte....*

—What on earth are you doing? said Sebastian as the lurching table sent half his papers on the floor.

—O, said Miss Reade who had leapt up suddenly. O, she said, sitting down again, with a white inscrutable face.

Some-one recalled that when the gendarme had come to take the old woman away, she had burst into tears and hung on the neck of her only beast, an eight months' old calf; and had cried in her funny dialect: O bon Diou, et mon p'tit viau . . . qui c'est-t-y qu'en aura soin?

—She'll get off, the bearded man said again. The girl was mad.

The young peasant said suddenly: She wasn't always mad.

—She's mad if the old woman says so. And she will. And she'll stick to it. They all do. And they all get off. Take the Blanche Monnier case, near Tours. Twenty years' starvation and torture, locked in a filthy cupboard. The father answers: but the girl is mad. Acquitted. Take little Andrée Belletier, near Le Mans, chained to a cellar wall for six years and with, among other injuries, an eye knocked out. But the child is mad. Acquitted. Two cases among hundreds. Among hundreds tried, and how many more undiscovered. They all say: mad. And they all get off. And so will the old woman: you'll see.

—That, said Madame pursing her lips. That, we do not know.

—Ach, said Käthe with round eyes. I am glad it was not me! And because Miss Reade looked so white she brought some fresh coffee without being asked; and Sebastian sent for a vieux marc and tipped it in and told her to drink it up, and they laughed at the faces she made; but her cheeks came pink again.

And Sebastian teased her: Lavinia, consider the egg. How elegant an egg. How clean an egg. How immediate, how bloodless, how impersonal a birth!

Which shocked Miss Reade considerably, but she smiled.

Sebastian it seemed was at work on a scene epitomising Walt Whitman's Adamic sons, who, chewing rhythmically and identical in shape and movement, poured from skyscraper doorways, straw hatted, waistcoatless, and spitting. Out they poured identical from identical doorways. A walking Greek chorus (Sebastian explained) conveying an impression of sameness, haste, well-washed teeth, and a cleaner Whitechapel. In the foreground, at the junction where Wall Street meets Lower Broadway, an impressive group, Presidents, Bankers, Congressmen, Kinema Magnates, and world-known American national characters, Big Bill Thompson, Al Capone, Flo Ziegfeld and his Follies, Otto Kahn, Mrs Aimée McPherson, Admiral Byrd, etc., is posed around a flag-draped plinth. It is the unveiling ceremony to the American Unknown Soldier. Or at least (Miss Reade gathered from the half-ear she lent to it) it was intended for the Unknown Soldier. There was a deathless fervour about the sententious patriotic phrases, mouthed nasally to the clockwork kicking of the Ziegfeld Follies Girls, gay as circus ponies; but somehow when it was unveiled it turned out to be the Tomb of the Unknown Dollar that fell so gloriously in the last great Wall Street War.

And now Madame was growing visibly angrier with the bearded man who having given the verdict, was passing-on to the summing up, throwing in here and there imaginary evidence and contradictory statements by the police, and generally by his misplaced animation, robbing her afternoon of dramatic significance.

O wailing Wall Street!

We shall see, we shall see, she thrust in his certainty like a sharp little knife. The echo mad! was like the cry of an ill-omened bird; and at intervals the young peasant with stubborn anger still put in a good word for the girl.

And Miss Reade was thinking that it is not enough. Not enough the little loyalties, the uncertain kindness, the vague sentimental impulse, with which mankind covers up the traces of its dirt; the drop of oil on the ocean of its ugliness.

O Cohens and coins and coins!

Not enough the unshed tear, the sudden charity, the pale-pink glow of good-fellowship, worn penny in the can of the world's misery.

And her heart was cold against Madame preening herself with that bright distinction peculiar to parrots and women of the French middle-classes. It seemed to her (irrationally but not without a grain of truth) that prinked in her satins with her child and dog, she should stand in the dock beside her compatriot. For surely both were accomplices in that they both were French

O profits of our fathers!

and had come from some thin-lipped Northern town, bringing their French-provincial bitterness, their overstrung nerves, and their shrill tempers to these slow-natured, pleasant, indifferent people who used to laugh till France taught them to giggle; who used to talk heartily square till France taught them to talk thinly pointed; and whose once-excellent roads, built by Germans, are left in ruins, while the great forests and passes of the Vosges are trenched and mined for instant destruction.

O Tomb of the Unknown Hero!

Only it was not enough the daily exchange of polite indifference; the rift of faint blue in an immensity of grey. It was not enough to mistrust one's neighbour only a little less than one mistrusted one's self. To bleat one's way into a state of grace before a fabled God and a state of fear before one's fellow man.

O last resting-place of the Unknown Dollar!

There should be the pure curves of stone about human faces (Lavinia Reade was thinking) as on Chinese and Assyrian statues with their benign and serious planes. Or the calm speechless eyes of the Greek thinkers, their brows packed tight and straight about their eyelids. One surprised a measure of it on the faces of these Alsatian peasants. A coolness of soul flowed from them effortlessly; a certain serenity of brow. For they did not deal with men but with the earth, which is less treacherous.

—And you haven't heard a word, said Sebastian, gathering up his papers.

—But surely I am coming to the first night, said Miss Reade with much presence of mind.

And now the motoring party which had been lunching in a far corner of the room was thanking Madame with enthusiasm; and was actually paying the bill without comment, though their speech was distinctly Parisian. And they were praising the painting which hung between the two windows. With some difficulty the date was read: 1744. Three soldiers with a bravura of gesture, drank to and ogled the servant girl, who stood before them in an abandon of rustic wiles. The painting had grace and an enchanting stupidity. It was exquisitely wrong where to have been right would have been to be null.

Miss Reade was glad they praised the painting, which gave

her immediate pleasure each time she raised her eyes to it. As though to make reparation for her thoughts in that strange way one has of feeling guiltily that one's mental comments have been overheard, she turned to Madame with a smile, saying impulsively:

—When I am rich, Madame, I shall return and buy that picture from you.

—Then you will have to buy the house, said Madame drily. For it is painted on the wall.

Were I a man, Lavinia Reade was thinking, I would love only men. I would not love women with their vacant chatter and soft ornamental bodies. I would not be charmed by womanly tempers when the coveted hat looked cheap and foolish. Nor treat her as a goddess for bearing me a child or two. To be only a woman is not worth very much; and the man who does not know it is a fool and deserves what he gets.

—Love between man and woman (Lavinia Reade was thinking) is an imperial thing. Leave it to Pericles and Aspasia, and Elizabeth and Robert Browning, and Abelard and Heloise. For the rest, I will feast and talk with my friend, and I will return to Xantippe when I must. For friendship is a thing enduring and safe. The middle course; the emotional Purgatory where one will never see God, nor even Gabriel's impassioned face. Only the lesser saints and an angel or two.

—Purgatory must be very like a small-sized Cathedral town, thought Lavinia Reade, and smiled to see herself elbowing plump Bishops and devout and maiden ladies to attend the weekly lantern lecture. Or coming down the High Street to change her book at the Lending Library and the lean Vicar, with sharp sad little cries, leading the ladies on small clipped wings out of her path to safety.

One clings to the end of things. The end of youth, the end of life, the end of a good dish, a good drink, a good book, a cigarette. Only the fountain endlessly jetting its tireless beads of sound from the mountain's hidden lip. But even that had ended, the legend ran, and once at a saintly prayer had poured wine lavishly as Christ poured his blood. Yet Buddha, said Miss Reade, who argued all things. Buddha needed no crucifixion! And drew-to the shutters.

The trouble was, being so very much alive among the dead. The born dead, the atrophied, the slow-dying. For dying is so slow a process, beginning imperceptibly in the soul and ending perceptibly enough in the stomach; and the walking behind the coffin may be an anti-climax by thirty years.

—Death may be a great adventure, said Lavinia Reade aloud. But life is a great gift! And threw herself on the bed. (If I'm sick, she thought, I shall simply ring for Käthe.)

O life is a great gift! For what right has one to each new day, to each new hour, but the right to accept and enjoy it? Yet so few seemed to know this, urgent though it might be. They seemed so dead, so slowly dying. They seemed disintegrating inwardly, with souls a little sick. The trouble, of course, was being so very much alive among so many dead. People resent it, thought Miss Reade. It is a kind of spiritual Bad Form.

All the unloved faces, the tight mouths, the nervous seeking eyes. It was not to the end of her affair with Harrion that she clung with such tenacity. She knew the signs. A fortnight's tears; a last effort at reconciliation; a few last arguments; and she was free again. Not so blatantly as that, of course. But as soon as the opportunity presented itself, free to love again. For it was essential to her to love the men with whom she slept. Essential to sleep, but essential also to love. For the illusion of love for one's bedfellow is important. It is the difference between pleasure and repeated exercise. Also it saved her from feeling humiliated when men left her. The essential she had had. What shocked her afresh was the ever recurring admission that there is an end. For it is not to the lover that one clings, but to the last of love.

Only one thing shocked and puzzled her. It was so real this revulsion of his, which made of her a laughing-stock and forced on her the arch leer of Madame Jonat and the gentle kindness of the youthful Käthe and the jocose humours of Sebastian. So that she could not turn from a window, nor look up as a door opened, but Madame's vulpine eye intercepted hers. And Sebastian looking up from his writing, murmured: It is not always the Foolish Virgin who sleeps . . . but the Bridegroom.

Miss Reade said coldly: Sebastian, you have all a woman's intuitive cunning. But none of her charm.

And now that to which she clung was nothing more tangible than a serenity of brow such as one surprised on the faces of these people at work in their fields; at rest before their doors. Once again one saw the seasons on the faces of one's fellow-men. One saw the young and serious, and the middle-aged and strong, and the old and humorous. A pleasure made more poignant by a tinge of sadness. For one had no right here. Who had no earth had no right here. Here was the dividing line between the ephemeral and the enduring.

A difference as real as the clerkly fear on the Londoner's face. That clerkly fear which is not a sudden fear, nor a tragic fear: but a small, an hourly fear. A fear of crossing roads, a desperate fear that the omnibus will not stop at one's stopping-place, that the train doors will not slide open at one's station; and that day-long fear of losing his job, which may be called the Londoner's supreme sensation. Under everything, eating at the heart of his restricted life, is the little cancer of the Lost Job. From the day he is accepted in his office and his clerkly life begins, throughout his pale amusements, the daily to-and-fro, marriage and the endless paying-off of house and furniture, the birth of his children;

binding all, held together by rheumatism and crowned by premature baldness, is the unspoken fear of losing his job. And there were millions upon millions of them, male and female, moving in and out of shops and banks and city offices, all with the furrowed foreheads, the unloved faces, the tight strained mouths of those to whom life is a happy vale of tears; an inglorious preparation for a better land; the echo of an invitation sent out from a hill-top: You must come and stay with my Father.

—The slave had at least the assurance that his master found him too valuable to lose, thought Lavinia Reade, turning her face to the wall to keep the afternoon sun from beating on her eyes.

Among the tricks which one's tired nerves can play is that it needs but the briefest hour to deny the ambitions of a lifetime. Perched on the wall of one's spirit the cock crows, and its derision has a hollow sound. One does not necessarily go out and weep at this betrayal of one's beliefs; or if one weeps it is only that one must go on living that in which one has ceased to believe.

—Old Willis, said Lavinia Reade with conviction but no enthusiasm, Old Willis will give me back my job.

And needless to say Miss Cullen would be there. One could travel the world round, through fire and shipwreck and famine and plague, and give birth to triplets by way of diversion between the monotony of adventures, and there, on one's return, seated on her swivel chair, in the small office behind the Reporters' Room on the second floor, snipping with large scissors the unalterable pattern of the London social round, ever-alert, ever-believing, ever-faithful, would one find again Miss Cullen, editress of the Woman's Page of the London *Daily World*.

Miss Cullen who believed. Miss Cullen who lived for her beliefs. Miss Cullen whose fervour had, to the onlooker, a pathos of childhood's unfaltering trust in a land of faery. Miss Cullen elongated and white faced, with pale undemonstrative hair, blue eyes misty with looking through rosy glasses at her coroneted world, scissors poised above *The Times* Social Column from which to weave her daily life's reality.

—And lovely Lady Skruschen looking not a day older than her radiant daughter.

—From Antibes I hear that Lady (Diddles) Blim.

—Where in the world could one match such exquisite youth and beauty as were to be seen gathered at the Duchess of Grates' dance for her niece, the enchanting Lady Deidre Dodo.

She wrote to a gay invisible melody. Sweet thrush on a thorny twig, she sang her hymn to the social sun, never doubting but that it would rise eternally and in ever increasing splendour.

And then for a brief space, and because work was short in the Reporters', there was thrust on her Miss Reade the undaunted, world-weary with the wisdom of twenty-two, an illegitimate child, two lovers, and a grievance at having to fill in the Silly Season on "woman's work" as she called it.

It was Miss Cullen who compromised. Finding she could not alter Miss Reade's cold inelegant style, she learnt to withhold comment and re-write it. Though not without a struggle.

—O but surely you ought to say that Lady Missles was looking levely?

—Ought I?

—O but didn't you think she was?

—I hadn't thought about it.

—O but how *could* you say such a thing! You *must* be joking. Ah think she's too-too levely. But then, everyone *does*. When she came out two years ago she was quate the leveliest thing ah've ever seen.

Miss Cullen frowned, re-wrote, sub-edited. Miss Reade returned to *Les Faux-Monnayeurs*.

—O you haven't said what Mrs Tally-Bounce was *wearing*.

—Which is she?

—O Mrs Tally-Bounce is quate too levely. You know her. Of

course you know her. With very fair hair and very dark eyes and quate petite and O always so exquisitely dressed.

—Probably red.

—But don't you *know*?

—Or green.

—O dear, O dear! Was it *red*? Or was it *green*?

—Put black and be safe. Tell her how too-too anything she looked in black. She'll not contradict you.

Miss Reade had been amazed. She found that social reporting entailed among other things standing in church porches with a crowd of eager gossip-page reporters note-booked and pencilled, taking down the names of those who attended smart weddings. Lacquey among the lacqueys she learnt to stand a little apart, inside the doorway, and to choose and dress the more celebrated names from an Agency report when back at her desk. She early found: call the lady beautiful and she will not protest at a mere colour scheme. So she stood within church doorways, in far thoughts of her own, watching her ardent colleagues name-gathering. And one day a Duchess rushed up to her with light pressure of the hand, crying: My dear, how well you're looking! Where *have* you been? I haven't seen you for ages! and gaily passed on. A not unnatural mistake, for she had an aloof, impudent dignity. And no note-book. Her colleagues who thought her cold and arrogant were momentarily non-plussed and smiled on her.

The sincerity of Miss Cullen touched and appalled her, whose quick mind saw too clearly the ways and means of journalism and its adherents. With a facility for words and a bright-seeing eye it was a game at which a child could play. Except for the crime reporters. For these she was loud and whole-hearted in her praise. Crime reporters and their long struggles with the authorities; often ending in the journalists solving the mystery to everyone's satisfaction and no one's acknowledgment.

So she would watch Miss Cullen living the lives of others by instalment; sipping the heady wine of titled ease by proxy. And she was kind to her. Or rather, she did not tease her more than she could help. Even on the mornings of gloom and resentment (for the affair with M'Hugh was going none too well) she would restrain her natural and now rather acid wit before Miss Cullen's guileless piety.

It was on one such morning that, writing of a party given the night before, on the occasion of some titled game-hunter's return to wife and family, an irresistible impulse made her add: *Or as the eighteenth-century lady's maid wrote home to her mother: M'Lord returned yesterday from the Wars and pleasured M'Lady three times before removing his boots.*

But could not. She looked long and thoughtfully at the back of Miss Cullen's pale undemonstrative hair and at the elongated neck bent rapturously above her devotions. The sight filled her with that faint but quite definite irritation which really gentle and selfless beings at times provoke in one. She sighed, frowned, surrendered. And the words from the succinct pen of the eighteenth-century lady's maid fell piecemeal in a twentieth-century waste-paper basket.

Yet it rankled; and coming back one afternoon from a musical reception held in a room the ornate gilt and satin and cupidon style of which she most particularly resented, she wrote of it as the type of room in which, two centuries since, they seemed for ever living in an amorous atmosphere of unmade beds and overturned chocolate cups.

Miss Cullen was delighted. She gurgled with joy; but it could not be used.

—Ah really think that *one* day you must *trey* and wraite a *book*, she breathed.

—Indeed? said Lavinia Reade discomfited.

Miss Cullen shared a flat with a schoolmistress friend who

had a sister; which sister was the one crease on the silken texture of her world.

—She is quate mād, said Miss Cullen in a hoarse whisper. So mād that she believes that if she *sat* on an *egg* she could *hatch* it.

—And has she tried? asked Lavinia Reade with interest; to be immediately non-plussed by Miss Cullen's pained surprise. It occurred to her that the one form of madness Miss Cullen would understand would be to sit on an egg and hatch the Holy Ghost. Or another such grave heraldic bird.

Meanwhile Miss Reade was piecing together a paragraph on correct precedence below stairs as still observed in a few great houses.

In referring to Lady Bogg's death, I might have mentioned yesterday that this robs of its chatelaine one of the few great houses the inmates of which still preserve below stairs all the ancient customs, so many of which have passed away since the war.

Thus the maids and valets of week-end visitors take the names of their masters and mistresses and take precedence accordingly in the servants' hall.

The maid of a duchess, for example, will sit upon the butler's right side, and if there be two duchesses in the party the maid of the older family of the two will take precedence.

Usually the butler only comes out of the house-keeper's room to take his pudding in the servants' hall. This is according to a long established custom, but on big occasions all the servants dine together, the butler sitting at the head of the table and acting as host, while the housekeeper acts as hostess.

Etiquette is infinitely more rigid than upstairs and the meals are conducted with a ceremony worthy of the Papal Court.

—I can't! cried Lavinia Reade throwing down her pen in sudden panic, her sense of the ridiculous more than usually outraged. I can't! *I can't* write any more of this wretched tittle-tattle!

—But Miss Reade, said poor Miss Cullen in her high, thin elderly voice. Miss Reade, it isn't just *tittle-tattle*. It is TEA-TABLE GOSSIP.

About this time M'Hugh struck her in the face going down the King's Road; and to his surprise she left him then and there. She gasped, broke in a run, rounded a corner, and that was the last he ever saw of her.

Observers have long been amazed at the discomforts the intolerant Englishwoman will face uncomplainingly abroad. He had fallen on her in a drunken rage one night in Madrid when she was seven months with child. He had struck her several times in Italy, where already he was becoming unreasonable. And once in Paris at Braccard's studio in the Rue Vavin, had decided to try throwing her out of the window. To all of which, this last impulse was as the gentlest expression of sudden rage. But it was also the King's Road, Chelsea. He had miscalculated the geographical significance of a blow. However drunk or irritated one may be, one does not strike an Englishwoman on her own doorstep.

Therefore, amazed, he watched her disappear as she raced home to pack (on a sudden impulse) a suitcase, secure sick-leave by telephone, and rush to catch a train, after agitated but none the less strict instructions to the patient Emily to let no-one in while she was away. (M'Hugh had a habit of living indefinitely on the hospitality of his friends.)

She found Evelyn in the garden of that enviable cottage of hers among the lesser hills of the restrained and gentlemanly Buckinghamshire.

—I never could understand what you saw in him, said Evelyn, later. His books are rubbish.

—A beard, especially a red beard, said Lavinia Reade, can be a powerful aphrodisiac.

—I never liked him.

—I don't like Jeremy, said Miss Reade ungraciously, dabbing at the home-made jam.

—Nor do I, particularly, said Evelyn. But I have such a horror of growing like my Aunt Elizabeth.

Miss Reade finished her tea in silence. She then said: As an erotic stimulant the fear of growing like one's Aunt Elizabeth should rank with the keeping-on of her boots by the German, the keeping-on of her corsets by the Viennese, and the clinging to her stockings and garters by the Parisienne.

Her friend looked up from her book, and smiled.

—And why not? she said pleasantly. We cannot all have naturally wide and hospitable legs.

—Wide and hospitable legs, said Miss Reade, no whit abashed, are the sign of a god-like and of a generous nature. Beware of all who keep their legs in any other way. Legs held together denote fear and servility. It is the symbol of the waiter, the servant, the Ambassador. Whereas legs apart and firmly planted are a proof of strength and independence. By their sign you may recognise the peasant, the Viking, the grande amoureuse.

—Suppose we went for a walk? said Evelyn, jumping up. For though not wishing to become like Aunt Elizabeth, she had an infallible belief in the efficacy of fresh air and exercise as a cure-all for eroticism.

But Miss Reade suddenly remembered that she was unhappy. She protested. She preferred, she said, to stay indoors and read Donne. Donne (she said) was the only poet who had ever made the Muse his mistress and taken her in to bed with him.

However, the house belonged to Evelyn, so they went for a walk.

But in the fresh air Miss Reade grew melancholy. She walked

with bent head, and stopping suddenly on the slope of a field, asked: What month is this?

Evelyn told her.

—Then we are a month late. Browning said one should be in England only in April.

Could this be May? in the valley the trees were wintry under their icing of Spring blossom. And this the sun: this chill, uneager disk, as though the least of all the Saints had lost his halo? And this the Spring: this unwilling birth whose tidings the larks bore hysterically aloft, while from distant fields the new lambs threw out their dismal stammer?

Evelyn was saying: This year it's been too perfectly awful! She was apologising, for she knew (though did not share) her friend's climatic distrust of her native land.

But Lavinia Reade made no answer. Indeed, she had not heard. She walked with bent head, in an angry abstract stride, lost in those thoughts which were the despair of her more circumspect and orderly minded friends. At last she said:

—Even Nature, in England, wears a fig-leaf.

A fig-leaf? Plus-fours! Not Ceres. Not the many-breasted Diana. No goat-footed god. But a well-washed, inhibited, and plus-foured Colonel plodding to the nearest golf-course. And the plus-foured Colonel takes no heed of sodden skies and flowerless hedgerows. He says: this, damme Sir, is England. This is not earth. This is land by the half-acre.

One felt it was. One felt, as one stared, that its sense of decency was being affronted. That being entirely sober, it knew its nakedness and was ashamed. It was eager to be clothed; to be cut in little lots and covered in an excrement of brick; to offer itself up in semi-houses for semi-people. The rounded shoulders of the hills were not for burdens of terraced vine, stiffened maize, or heavy corn. They were for villas back to back, a latched gate, a strip of green, a blue lupin or two. Not yet; but soon. In ten years' time when London, that breeding-ground of clerks, had worried its dust-heap of suburb a further thirty miles.

Perhaps I've been too long abroad, she thought; remembering (particularly) a farmhouse, long, two-storied, coloured the familiar etruscan red-ochre, its windows outlined in bands of pinkish lime, lost in the ebb and flow of the hills above Petroio. Tuscan speech is like incense in the mouth. Goat's milk has a heavy acrid taste. One mixes *ricotta* with rum and sugar. Guilletta of the golden face and classic brow brings fruit to the table, sighing: *fa baldo nella basa*. About the doorways cheerful old women gossip melodiously, and work the long ribbons of leghorn straw to be sent to Florence. There are two streets; one walks up the one which leads to the other. Tuscan peasants with naked feet pass among their vines and fields, for there a man's feet are not white and pitiful but are sunk in the warm earth like stalks with roots.

Yet this, too, was May: this discreet reflection of an ardent act; this onlooker at Nature's festival. The sky was long low-lying cloud. The earth cold and desolate. There was a something inhibited and unwilling about it all. Only the birds, twittering like mice in the heavenly wainscotting. And they seemed foreigners. They were noisy and gay and alive; like the Italians in Soho. And as such were not so much part of the scene as tolerated by the restrained and gentlemanly countryside, the barrier-like hedges, the stony fields. Could it be that in England there must be no display of vitality even on the land and sky? Life's expression must not be extravagant and even Nature's voice may not be raised? All is superior and self-conscious. All things merge. The sun-less tradition of the earth is one with its inhabitants. The people are subdued and the fields are subdued. The people are grey and tweedy, and the fields are grey and tweedy. And over both blows the cold breath of primness and gentility and fear; fear of nakedness, of exuberance, of life.

—Of all the earth England cooled first!

Miss Reade looked back, startled. It rang so clearly in her ears that she stood still. Some-one had spoken. But Evelyn lagged behind and was calling to her dog. Realising that the words were her own, she smiled; her heart fluttered in harmless vanity, for she loved the ruthless summary in a sentence. She looked up and around at the chill and the grey, and repeated slowly and aloud: *Of all the earth England cooled first.*

—Evelyn, she called. O Evelyn! Listen to this....

—He won't COME ! Evelyn yelled back. It's no USE. He's after RABBITS !

But by the time Evelyn caught her up, she had ceased distorting a wintry landscape to fit a sudden nostalgia for Spring on a Tuscan hillside. She was leaning on a gate, staring at a cow. The cow (needless to say) was staring back. Her expression was benign. Miss Reade's was hostile. The cow chewed, gently moving her soft and juicy nose. Miss Reade's fine nostrils were distended in surprise and distaste. She seemed never before to have seen a cow, or to have understood its purpose. Such a voluminous, pink, veined, all-too-human appendage appalled her as a source of nourishment. The fat pink fingers were obscene as a fat, soft, money-loving hand. Confronted by her wetnurse the squeamish citizen revolted. Too near a view of such mammiferous bounty, alarmed her. This then, with its pendulous pink bag, was the source of civilised life. To this swaying breast (for the cow not having to understand sights with her mind, had lost interest in staring, and had returned to her food) to this swollen unappetising fount, the modern mother brought her new-born babe. Here was a field of them, ripping-up with small sharp sound the fresh grass, to be dropped foaming into pails, to be warmed in tens of millions of bottles and held to puling mouths. All this tearing up of grass by these poor patient beasts on whose broad backs the modern woman had shifted her intimate maternal duty.

At last she broke a long silence.

—I am like that, she said thoughtfully.

—I suppose you are, said Evelyn. Only the cow is less emotional. And, of course, never argues.

—Yet I am right, said Miss Reade slowly. And you are wrong. I am old-fashioned. I admit it. I need men. And I need children. I am the human cow. But you are the modern woman. You dislike children. You do not really care for men. Where the fear of Aunt Elizabeth has led you, instinct has led me. Yet one should function correctly, said Lavinia Read with finality. So I am right.

But Evelyn would have none of it. She was coldly derisive. She denied that the act of love was for anything as dull and limited as the mere reproduction of self. She called children the compensation of the unloved. That the act of love should be for anything but pleasure (she said) was both immoral and unthinkable. Women who desire only to be mothers should be mechanically fertilised. Let them be placed apart and tended and graded like cattle. Let them admit their cow-like vocation. Let them be contented by the yearly child. But let them leave the passionate act to the passionate.

Meanwhile the anonymous wet-nurses of the citizens continued grazing peacefully, unperturbed by a distressed onlooker's sudden conversion to beer.

But soon the earth grew warm, serious, productive. The hysteria of Spring was past. The cuckoo's anvil-echoing died down. One lay on one's back in deep clover, in an infinitude of moons which, when picked, told Continental time.

And one thought of M'Hugh who (as Evelyn said) wrote indifferent books; and of how love may become a habit; and of how restless one can be, deprived of it. Not that his books were so very poor. Certainly, they sold.

To pick up a book by M'Hugh was mentally akin to dancing around a maypole. It had charm, a gentle humour, and was instinct with the very breath of English country life. It was also sad, and filled with yeoman farmers who seemed never (until this book began) to have imagined, much less seen, a patch of land other than their own, and off which they were about to be turned. Either they could no longer make it pay, wherein it became a grim battle between the new town and the home of their forefathers; or the sons became slowly mad, through hereditary taint; the cottager's lass was brought to shame by the head of the house; the proud daughter ran away with the commercial traveller. Life for them was monotonously dour and hard. Early M'Hugh seemed to have understood that peasants in literature must suffer, and suffer much. Withal that intoxicating perfume of roses welling in cottage gardens; the thatched roof and straggling street; the light easy touch of dialect; the pewter mugs banged on wooden tables; and the wide wild eyes of love betrayed.

His work was a never-ending source of wonder to one who knew him so well as did Lavinia Reade. The man himself (she had often thought) was so much more arresting in his brutal insensitiveness, that it seemed a pity he should not make use of it in his work. Why, in that little inn in Barcelona, before they had been living together three months, he had insulted her so savagely that even the sailors sitting there had had to ask him to be more gentle to her. What a good story that would have made, though in her case he had not noticed the wide wild eyes. And how often had he not threatened to return home, leaving her without money? Not that he was insensitive to suffering. The sight of a beaten child or a kicked dog could put him to exquisite torment, and to tirades of vengeance.

And how indignant he had been the day of the bullfight when she had laughed and clapped her hands. He had wanted the whole thing stopped. It was revolting. It was barbaric. It was the refinement of torture. He sat withdrawn in anger and disgust. And she had laughed and called it cardboard. Lovely gaudy cardboard. It was Punch and Judy played with bulls and men. They sat high up, on the tightly packed benches among the garlic and the sweat and the orange peel; and all around them the people yelled in their brazen ciccalous voices. She had thought it superb, the lithe mastery of the men; the silken tricked-up insolence of the show. And once when the crowd rose and shouted, she rose and shouted with it, at the blood and the colour and the sun and the cool impertinence of a waving cloak. Straight, swift, sure, and beautiful! Thus should one kill a bull. Thus should one take a woman.

Afterwards he could hardly bring himself to speak to her. Yet he called the child: your brat; and the week it was born he went away. He had gone to buy some cigarettes, and had not returned, leaving her with the few shillings so often threatened. She felt very ill and, unable to ask for a doctor in understandable Spanish, went to bed in that terrifying stone room with the stone floor. And would have gone on lying in bed had not the woman of the house bustled in and throwing up a jet of words like the ceaseless twanging of a guitar, had got her out of bed and sat her between two chairs with a basin beneath; and after a timeless flow of pain it was over, and the woman was laughing and washing the child, and she was back in bed again. And at the end of a week M'Hugh walked in, having bought his cigarettes. He was surprised to see the child. He behaved as though it were an immaculate conception; or as though such things were announced and achieved by incantation, or a form of black magic between witches and women. Later he said that he had gone away because he could not bear to see her suffer.

—That was a mistake, she had told him gently, with that fine candour of hers. One should know every thing that is life. It would have been useful to you.

But mention of his work was the unvarying signal for a display of pained anger on his part. Here was an exposed and acutely sensitive nerve. His work was sacred and above discussion. It must not be tarnished by careless tongues. It was the Pure Woman of the poet's dream. Reality was the harlot.

Besides, was this a time to speak of work? What work? How? When? Weren't they about to be deafened day and night for the next six months?

But if this was an excuse it failed. The infant was so quiet that he both terrified and fascinated Miss Reade, who also had anticipated six sleepless months. He lay peacefully self-communing, self-absorbed, drawing on a store of timeless memories which seemed to amuse him, for he chuckled a great deal. Mother and son were attracted to one another from the start. The admiration was mutual. Possibly because they had the same habit of absorbed staring and laughter came readily to both of them. She would bring a book and would read aloud and charm him with her light, eager voice:

Busie old foole, unruly Sonne,
Why dost thou thus,
Through windowes, and through curtaines call on us?

He liked that. Or:

Outcrept a sparrow, this soules moving Inne,
On whose raw armes stiffe feathers now begin.

But all that he knew, the Emperor, and the Post-Horse, and the Mucheron, the spider, the shee wolf, the embryon fish. He slept.

Often she sat bent over the table in the shadow, with her back to him; and sometimes when she was finished would come and read it to him. One day she read: *And here ... in 1452 ... the son of God was born. For if God Himself is Omniscience, then none has ever come so near to Him as has Leonardo da Vinci.* This time he not only chuckled, he waved his legs and waved his fists; and his mother was so pleased that she kissed him all over and dropped two large tears on his head in playing.

When M'Hugh came in she told him that Bill would be among the greatest living scientists, and made him watch the child's involuntary response to the word: Vinci.

But Bill was staring sideways at his father.

—And he has the scientist's unwavering eye, said Miss Reade, disappointed.

Why the hell, M'Hugh wanted to know, did she keep on calling the creature Bill. Why not Joe? Or Ed? or Jim? He was working himself up; it was a sore point.

—Bill for Billingsgate, said Miss Reade solemnly, though she had only just thought of it. His father had the manners of a fish porter.

M'Hugh wanted him christened John Andrew Robert after an only (and rich) uncle in Devon; and wanted him christened at once. The rich uncle was not now on speaking terms with his unspeakable nephew, but on hearing of John Andrew Robert and the honour conferred on him, the effect must be magical. He might even offer to adopt the brat and pay its expenses.

But Bill's mother was adamant. She agreed, she said, with the Red Indians. When Bill had shown himself worthy of a name he should receive one and be finally and officially christened. But not till then.

Moreover, the fair name of a future scientist must not be smirched by a cowardly dream of a penitent uncle in distant Devon. From here (for she stood on the balcony looking at the painted boats gliding on a green sea, and at the idling of the dark-skinned men in the toy, white-gleaming harbour) the thought of

Devon was as remote as it was fantastic. And she told him why. It was not to the Bills of this world that one gave the names of revered uncles. Strangely enough these had but to appear, to turn avuncular hearts to granite. But somewhere in Devon, midway (socially) between the Hall and the Village, in a simple tennis frock, dewily innocent as though from the pages of one of his own novels (which she kept under her pillow, and wept upon, her underlip between her teeth) She waited. She had heard dark and unmentionable things of her hero's private life; but faith was beautiful; and it must be that one day He and She came face to face.

—And you shall. In time. First the desire will come to you to shave that handsome beard which now makes people turn and wonder who that may be. Which will compel you to tie a neat bow under your chin. Which means shirts of a more-seemly pattern. And even a new suit. And a ticket from Waterloo (for the fight will be over!) to the land of Drake and the Armada. A jocular Uncle. A girl in a tennis frock. At the sight of so much real Innocence your apathy will drop from you: for a simple tennis frock on a Devon lawn is a modern maiden's Belt of Chastity. And later think how uncomfortable you will be in the dead of night when the young mother sleeps, at the thought of another John Andrew Robert who has no right to the proud name of M'Hugh. And you will grow pale and neurasthenic wondering when the blackmailing will begin; just as in your books. And for how much? No, no. Let him leave Uncle John Andrew Robert till true repentance was on him and he decided to settle down. And let him for the moment leave Bill alone. For Bill ever to have a name he must make it.

And it was so true that M'Hugh was angrier than ever. He ground his teeth on his pipe, waved his arms helplessly, vaguely, to take in the child, himself, the sea, the sky, her, the white road to the harbour, and said between his teeth, and practically in tears, that everything, everything was a joke to her. She seemed to have no decent feelings. It was terrifying. Where any real woman would cry, she laughed. She scoffed. She ridiculed. She had no heart. What did he want with his damned uncle but his money, and a decent sort of name for the child, and perhaps someone to look after it.

She had put an arm in his and her head against his shoulder, and said: Dearest, what is there to be serious about? We're only poor once! (and even as she had said it, she knew how wasted it was. But how Rollo would have loved that remark!)

The six months past, they boarded a fruit steamer in Malaga which eventually set them down in Naples, and from there walked as fancy took them, vaguely toward Rome and Florence. The infant wore nothing but an enormous red cotton handkerchief knotted round him like a workman's dinner-pail, which made him no trouble at all to carry, and when they came to a village Miss Reade would make straight for the piazzetta and splash him kicking into the fountain, and the women would come tumbling out of doorways with sharp cries and uplifted hands, wailing: *Il poveretto! Aië, mamma mia, il poveretto!* So shocked they were to see a baby treated like a husband's shirt.

When at last they returned to England, Bill was taken to Cornwall and duly christened with names befitting a future world-scientist, and left at the farmhouse which had been so highly recommended. Already Bill had the thinker's impersonal outlook. He made scarcely any fuss at parting. He was intent on studying a hen and some chickens. Miss Reade wondered would she miss him at all; and in the train it occurred to her how pleasant it must be to be old: old and out of reach.

On the way home she stopped the taxi-cab in the King's Road and bought an armful of tulips, and some mushrooms, and a bundle of asparagus. But M'Hugh was gone to the Ballet with Charles and Edwina. The note added self-righteously that he had put the cat outside.

But it is good to be alone in those moments in which living seems suddenly a thing external, an effort made under pressure; or as though one had been seized against one's will and hurried down turnings one did not wish to take. The glow from the lights on the Embankment outlined the room, the plane trees below, the water's edge, the benches for the homeless and the lovers. All over the world people were drawing their souls out through their mouths. All over the world were farmhouses where children crowed among the hens and chickens. All over the world little blue postmen hurried down streets on their last rounds, dealing joy and pain with an impartial hand.

And she had stared in the faces of the flowers she had bought, and had thought how one does not lose one's innocence with one's virginity, but when first one learns how treacherous people are. It seemed there was a rape of the soul which was of all things the most horrible, because without beauty and without passion. An ugly, solitary, spinsterish act.

I thought you would be ill, Käthe was saying. You looked so white. I thought you would be ill.

She had opened the shutters to let in more air, and hovered anxious and sympathetic.

Miss Reade said nothing. Partly that she found the remark unnecessary; partly that the taste in her mouth was unpleasant. She steadied herself a moment on the edge of the bed, then went to the window and leant on the sill. The warm air played on her face. But it was unreal, too bright, the sudden sight of shouting children tearing over cobbles, the aged houses tilting at each other, the swaying ascent of spires, roofs, hills, to the sun. She went back and sat on the bed, her head on her arms.

Meanwhile Käthe was busy at the wash-hand-stand; but

more busy in her mind wondering how to show that she understood these things; that she knew quite well that to be sick like this for no reason one must be wearing a wedding ring.

At last she said: When my mother was sick she always had strong black coffee without sugar, afterwards. And she had eight.

But Miss Reade must have missed the subtlety, for she neither blushed nor frowned. On the contrary, she was extremely grateful and said: Then suppose you go and bring me some, and we'll see whether your mother was right.

So the disappointed Käthe meekly put the finishing touches to the room and hurried away to the kitchen. For how does one resist a smile that is like the mutual sharing of some secret joy?

When next Miss Reade looked up there Käthe stood like an Annunciation angel bringing coffee, but no sugar. And as she drank, Käthe watched with eyes wide, as though hypnotised. And as she drank Miss Reade watched Käthe and thought how Nature is more tittivating than any woman's dress-maker in the matching of earth and man: black hair and eyes with figs and black grapes: straw-coloured hair and blue eyes with white grapes and corn; three steps backward with head on one side, professionally pursed mouth, and a slow satisfied nod.

But it was more than Käthe could bear, the suspense, the being stared through as though she were not there.

—You are not afraid? she whispered.

—Of what? asked Miss Reade startled. Of dying, breathed Käthe.

Ach, to look so good and yet to laugh at Sin and Death as though there were no God above! Käthe turned from pink to red. Miss Reade stopped laughing.

She said that it was not nearly as bad as people pretended, and warned her against believing all the silly stories she heard. And suddenly feeling she might have said too much, amended: At least, I can't believe it is!

Not, she felt, that she had anything to conceal, but out of deference to Käthe's sensibilities. It was always as well to remember Sebastian's witty dictum: I never lie. I amplify or I restrict Truth.

She added pleasantly: Besides, look how strong and healthy I am.

And all at once like a dimpled bursting cloud Käthe was pouring her life story, her married sister, her brothers, an old father, a dead mother, the young man they were urging her to marry at once, saying that a year's courting was enough for any girl these hard times. Käthe pouted and tossed her head. For they were marrying her a little (though not altogether) against her will. And she was frightened. She pretended that it was because farm work is long and difficult, and there would be enough to do on her parents-in-law's farm. She spoke resentfully. She seemed to think that she was being pushed into marriage to help with the potatoes, yet all the while was fascinated and half-angry, unwilling and eager for the day when like a piece of furniture and with no more ceremony than the bridal sheets she must spread herself out and render up her possessions, the woman's placing of all her cards on the table, the giving of the only thing she has to give, except help on the farm and the cooking of meals.

Trapped under the confidential cloud-burst Miss Reade sat marvelling that already six years were past. Eighteen! All that part—the Käthe part—Rollo had had. And how willingly, how thoughtlessly given. My Lord was like a flower upon the brows of lusty May. O, Blake knew! Rollo whose very letters one remembered years afterwards, as though read yesterday, as though still lying half-open on one's lap.

Nice, nice people. I am exhausted. The Countess is more beautiful than I thought. The Countess is more cultured than I thought. She loves Rossetti and particularly the statue of Peter Pan. Art is in the family. Her mother was exhibiting in Liverpool with the British Amateur Water-colour Society....

That, of course, in the days before he was given to painting sleek women as waterfalls of light and colour; acclaimed by the many, mourned by a few early friends who had watched his downfall. That, in the golden days when living could be so plain that it was difficult to think high any more, but by a happy trick one was able to retrieve the shillings one had just dropped in the gas-meter, and spend them on innumerable and unnecessary little jugs of cream, which (did you ask him how he got them) he'd say: . . . ssh. I milked a mouse!

Perhaps Käthe was right. Perhaps one would die. For if death is a sleep, what death was there for a woman but death in childbed? And then, how eager, how more exacting life would become if one could know the day and hour of leaving it. Then only murderers met death bravely with senses alert, facing the inevitable. The newsboys shout, the decent citizen buys a paper, reads with horror, pities the wretch, and, still reading, falls under the first 'bus that thunders by without sounding its horn. That was not death, but an accident. Death should not be made a thing of chance or blackmail, but the body's leaping at the struggle of old and new, with for the vanquished (the woman) the reward of unending sleep. With the first pangs should come a slow gasping for breath; with the first new cry, the death rattle.

Käthe was saying nervously: . . . perhaps . . . now he'll marry you. And blushing yet again.

—Who? said Miss Reade, returning sharply to life.

—. . . the tall one, of course. . . .

But Miss Reade said abruptly, struggling between irritation and a desire not to hurt the girl's feelings, that there was no question of marriage. Adding also that she had no desire or intention of ever marrying.

—Never, she said decisively, as Käthe exclaimed. At least not with the men I seem fated to meet. They are too clever. And clever men are neurotic and unhappy; and about as easy to live with as precocious children. All the men you see downstairs, Käthe, are one-half women. Just as silly, and even more vain.

So Käthe understood that it was all a joke and giggled: Then what is a man!

—Otto, said Lavinia Reade. Otto is a man. And all those you see at night coming home from the fields. Those are men. They work with arms and muscles as a man is meant to do. You will find them carrying their children around in their arms; but not their emotions. The men you see downstairs, Käthe, said Miss Reade, warming to her task, do not need wives and fields and children. They need an audience. Without an audience they are as lost as a pretty woman without a mirror. Or as clowns in an empty tent. No; that is unfair to the clown. He contorts only his face. He can hang his grin on a nail with his tights and spangles. He can go home and rest, drink his soup and smoke his pipe, and grumble at his wife because his toes stick through his socks. But these leap and tumble in their minds, twist and posture in their hearts, and for them there is no rest. They are those enchanting prismatic toys one bought as a child, shaking bright patterns from their tongues and brain; and at each new pattern you must clap your hands and praise it. Then they are happy. For they must never be allowed to think that their pattern is not the best pattern, even though in their hearts they may know it is not the right pattern. Or that the sounds they weave with their tongues are not the strangest sounds; even though they be without soul or substance: but just a little argument. Or they grow melancholy. They wilt. They even die. But even if they throw themselves in the river, my child, it is only that they rush out to embrace their own reflections.

Miss Reade stood up and went to the window.

—Praise them, sl-laugh with them, she said, but never marry them.

Below in the sunlight old men sat still as alligators, absorbing the hours. Children fell in and out of doorways. A beribboned cock strutted. A hen with gracious feathered curves led her fidgeting chicks with sounds like heavy single drops, drip-dripping on a stone.

—Come and look, said Lavinia Reade:

A fat little boy of about four with stuffed pink legs, struggled across the market-place, kicked and pinched another small boy, tore some form of toy from him, and struggled back again. A howl of rage and defeat went up, very like those rancid notes with which sopranos announce that the end is near. Smaller children gathered and stared; slightly older sisters appeared from nowhere, surrounded the victim, hugged it tightly in thin arms as though the screams must cease by pressure. Meanwhile the thief was out of sight, though there was much vague pointing and shouting of threats, and at last the screamer, whom only justice would appease, was led away on small unsteady legs and a bodyguard of angry voluble little girls, in the direction the enemy supposedly had taken.

Käthe grinned. She, too, had comforted small fat brothers, unbuttoned them, spoiled them, bullied them, and wiped their noses; all better fun than playing with dolls. She said:

—This year there were two young storks, but the parent-birds have killed one.

—How do you know?

Everyone knew said Käthe. Because they always did. Each time there were two, one was killed. And each year before they flew away they gathered in a field and killed all the weak birds, young and old, whom they thought unfit for the journey. O, yes, they did! They beat them with their beaks, like this. And sometimes one found two or three dead storks in a field, and then one knew that they had gathered there before going away. But there were not so many now. They had been frightened by the guns during the War and had stayed away, and besides they got shot at so much, crossing Italy. Weren't they *funny* things? Standing always on one leg, high above the houses and peering down their long noses; and looking so proud! as though it was too much for them even to touch the earth at all. Just like.... And here Käthe blushed once more. But she was a simple soul, with no sense of servility, who thought that having poured out her own story fully entitled her to enter yours. Just like (she said) the tall man who was always running off by himself . . . when here you are . . . and here everything is . . . so happy and so alive . . . but then one looked at him and it was just like the stork standing on one leg, and hating having to stand even on that.

What would be the good of showing annoyance? Besides, the description was so apt. One leg on the earth, and even that was too much for him! She recalled his back, immune, indifferent, hurrying out of sight in the early sunshine.

On, on and on, went Käthe, a torrent of loyalty and partisanship. And all at once Miss Reade found that watching the silly gentle creature babbling away she could not hear a word she said, but only saw her mouth opening and shutting. It was not the first time this had happened to her. Often it was as though sudden intensity of feeling could paralyse her eyes and ear drums, so that she could not see or hear the thing or person who had caused it. And yet she knew she smiled. For there was a queer strain of compassionate indolence in her, so that even in moments of almost hysterical revulsion or boredom Lavinia Reade rarely said the unkind, unnecessary things she might have. A trait which misled many people. But it was only an indolent helplessness. A be good to people. Be kind to them. One sees them but once. Time is so short and its aftermath so long. Say the things they want you to say. And so she thanked Käthe for her help, and said that now she would lie down awhile, and even that she thought she heard some-one calling downstairs and that Käthe had better run; and no sooner was the door shut on the grateful creature than Miss Reade found the tears trickling down her face. For, of course, he had left her. She saw it all clearly, standing at the window while Käthe compared him with a stork. He was gone and would not come back. She saw the train bearing him away, tearing off in an unknown direction with stubborn, foolish secretiveness. So she stood and wept tears that came without effort. All that she knew of them was that they ran down her cheeks. Modern Leda mourned without passion her one-legged stork. She wept, as an hour since she had been sick, meaninglessly. She was not hurt or angry. She was pregnant and so she was sick; she was alone and so she wept. Though it was now too late to weep and quite useless. The real tears had all been shed four weeks ago. And the last. But she felt young and abandoned and empty and at a loss; and what she had feared was not important at all, and really concerned her no more. But it had happened, and so the tears ran down her cheeks as she stared from the window and thought how foolish to waste such an afternoon indoors and that she would go out for a walk.

When, as it happened, he was not gone at all, but at the moment Miss Reade, staring from the window, saw him borne away in foolish and relentless haste, he was somewhere between Muttersholz and Wittisheim, sitting on one of those red-stone benches, half-torii half-druid altar, which line at intervals the Alsatian roads. He was watching a stork, grave enchanted bird, stooping for food in a field. Until a shy straw-haired child who had come down the road with a man and had crept up to stare at him sitting there motionless and unreal, distracted him; but as he turned and looked at her she retreated wildly to the waiting man and held on to his hand and stumbled away, pressed anxiously against familiar legs.

It seemed his life had been but a magnified day. Behind him days stretched by repetition into years and years, by a monotony of hours, habits, and repeated acts, dwindled once more to a day.

Constancy of habit to this tyranny of hours had meant a succession of timed wakings, baths, shaves, breakfasts, work, home-comings, sleep; to wake again to baths, shaves, breakfasts, work, home-comings, sleep. The year-long shuttling between office and home, three hundred and sixty-five breakfasts punctually set, eaten and digested, to each hour of each day its act, in a year three hundred and sixty-five times performed, in ten years three thousand six hundred and fifty times performed; add on; then look back. The answer is a day.

And in these years reduced by routine, by the solemn precision of habit to a few hours, hopes, desires, frustrations, loomed no larger than minutes; or were mere irritants, straws dropped across an insect's mile-long path. For life (he found) is measured by the breakfasts one has eaten rather than by the emotions one has used or avoided; and it was not whether these breakfasts were pleasant or palatable, wanted or unwanted that remained; but the fact of having sat down to them. For in the end detail is eliminated, habits merge in the whole, the whole becomes a lifetime, the lifetime becomes a day.

Possibly they distort some part of one in childhood. They always do. A bleakness of female caution, an excess of male enthusiasm; bleatings, fears, regrets. Regular hours form regular habits. Regular habits ensure long life. A matter of Bleeding Gums and Unsuspected Constipation. But then Harrion never could read advertisements. They reminded him of his mother, whose lips had parted only in things moral and offensive; of himself, a pale thin child, ashamed of his pallor; of his father, even in that mediocre grey-slate town among the most self-effacing, even in his work dependent on the wills of others; and such dull unimaginative wills that could never hope to be queried or disputed: *that* sort (as his wife never tired of pointing out) went to those fortunate beings who kept their own carriage.

If! If if if if. But all the breakfasts had been eaten. Possibly the capacity for emotion is like the capacity for food: gorge and the stomach throws it back. Only a certain measure of affection is given to each: a mother or an aunt, an adopted son, a canary. Beyond that the spent effort cannot be flogged. There comes an end to desire. Life recedes. One is washed up at last on some cold peak of inner solitude. For the bitter parable of Eden is that one first must eat the fruit before finding at its core the dry-rot of indifference.

Harrion looked down. An ant exploring his hand as though it were the road to Lhasa, climbed hills, fell among hairs, and struggled to safety in a valley between fingers; and was no sooner safe than again was up hills, into hairs, panicked, and was safe again. He bent forward, hung his hand over a blade of grass and watched the busy creature lose itself in the meadow's trembling undercurrent.

Unbroken by hedges the vast plain flowed evenly to the very edge of the tree-bordered road, like a grassy sea meeting sand. Fields stretched as far as the eye could follow, stopped only by hills spread in shells across the sky, with here and there a glint of village roof and strip of tilled land. Warm and slumbrous the outer edges dissolved in a mist of heat. A white horse with crimson ear-caps stood with restless tail and stamping hoofs in the shade of an apple tree heavy with its gallant burden.

Who can explain why a child falling under a lorry can make of a lifetime a matter of hours half lived? Perhaps because a child is an innocent untroubled little thing symbol of some lost state of grace. There is no harsh edge to its voice; no memories in its laughter; and to the touch it is as though one put an arm through a branch of apple blossom. Perhaps because a child is oneself reborn, and one will take greater care of this second more precious self; this other chance one dared not hope one had deserved.

From afar and from a church turret graceful as a gazelle came a hint sound of bells, needlessly telling the hour to those who lay beneath it with their lives crossed out. A scented wind gathered up the sounds and odours of the clover. In the nearest meadow a poplar stood above its shadow, stereoscopic against the sky. White butterflies rose on agitated waves bringing tidings to the flowers; and a large dark bee assaults a dandelion that bends under its weight, grips with amorous knees, opens petals, exposes secret places, and releases it, swaying; flies to the next, deflowers them all, a very Mahomet among the virgins.

To-morrow he would leave, would walk away, the last human contact would be broken; he would be free. Since now he could no longer look at his fellow-men, but could look only through and beyond them. It was as though when he looked flesh and blood fell away and he saw a scaffolding of bone, the outline of a skull. In an awful alertness of perception, suspended, apart, he saw the decay in all living matter, the long decomposition above ground which is called life; its fascination, its futility. It pleased him to find that in a walk he could hear the skeleton's dragging of its joints. The child who had crept up to stare at him, had stumbled away as a small heap of bones dancing on strings, crookedly unsure of its legs. Yet people went to extraordinary and pathetic lengths to gain such power as had come to him unsought. They drank, drugged, prayed, in efforts to release, to drown a will and turn consciousness to fluidity. To no purpose. For the drunkard returns to reality only to drink again to escape it; and drink and morphine remain the drugs of the sentimentalist. But indifference is the realist's drug. It does not obscure, it clarifies. It sets life in *relief* and one is borne above and beyond the limits of its bleak mediocrity to chill distances from whence there is no return. Never again will one shrink from that most terrifying of all earthly things: the human eye. One has gone beyond the retina's prying reach. Eyelids are no longer barriers one feared to face; for they close on no-thing; an airpocket; two bony cavities; twin hollows, void and meaningless as the grave.

As though to distract him a stream crossing the field with the small rustle of a silk petticoat quickened its step; and suddenly the air was filled with a busy passing of messages between birds, and as suddenly was so still that one heard that faint whisper in the tops of trees in which peasants at work in fields hear an angel speaking, or the prophecies of saints. Unheeding the meadow shimmered intensely alive and eager in its musical undercurrent of heavy clover, its hoard of new-minted buttercups, blue salvias, ox-eyed daisies, purple campanulas, and the soft pink spire of the field polygonum.

What a weaving, a meadow! How lavish a texture of untroubled hours! What a mirror of that brief moment in which one grows self-absorbed as a field in flower. All the sights and sounds of childhood, when staring in a pond is more than a wizard's staring in space, and the water-spider's giant stride, and the water-beetle's metallic gleam. A meadow is one's first innocence. A meadow is a childhood's memory.

From the incline where she sat looking down on the village (surely the birds had built these houses, so warm, so neatly fitted in the hollows) Lavinia Reade stopped poking the ground with her stick, raised her head and said aloud: I want her to be a gay young thing! I shall call her Bernardine.

For she could not rid herself of the belief that it was good to be alive and happiness enough to be sitting on the earth crying, when one might be sitting under it with no tears to shed, and nothing to be sad about, and no possibility of laughing or wondering what could happen next, or ever again. For let who would call death the great adventure, life (Lavinia Reade decided) life is a great gift.

A decision that had spoilt more than one dramatic moment. As on the day Rollo left her and intent on suicide she had sat down to write a will, only to find that after an hour's tearful staring in the gas fire she had written:

And I leave my spine to the Gas Light and Coke Company,

and had begun to laugh and unable to stop had gone for a walk, and had laughed all down the Embankment till she came to the aged mummified woman in the vast shining car, taking the air under the trees beside the river; the manly chauffeur pacing with the pekingese. And she had paused, shocked back to life at what seemed a bag of putrid flesh, yellow as its gold, pretending (for it could only have been pretending) that it breathed and felt the cool air on the face it turned so sightlessly to the water. One had thought the Bolshevists invented such things for their posters. And not ten steps away sat the man stubbornly staring at the pavement with that cold look the underfed retain even on the mildest days, beside him on the bench his three little girls, with impertinent little Cockney faces, the youngest of whom he was shielding with his battered coat, while she munched a large crust of dry bread.

And Lavinia Reade who not an hour since was on the verge of suicide but for a mis-timed sense of the ridiculous, had walked on thinking of the rich and of how they die and putrify among their possessions; and of how inferior they almost always are to their beasts and servants; riders to their horses, the driven to their chauffeurs. And of the poor, who are invariably superior to their clothes and environment; so much so that one never wishes to harm or attack them, but only to take away and replace their poor mean clothing and their ugly wretched homes.

A poultry farm, she decided. All one had to do to get hundreds of chickens was to give them tea-leaves and potato-peel (or was that pigs?) and they laid eggs and sat on them, which meant more chickens and double as many eggs. Then one added cows, for all *they* needed was a field and they too (and so willingly) gave you double as many cows. Which makes hundreds of gallons of milk and thousands of eggs; lorryloads of milk and eggs for all the London poor, because it must all be given away, as in a perfect world flowers would be given away (but flowers one would add later); everything should be a gift, for it was unthinkable that people, poor people who shielded their children with battered coats, should be made to pay for food, particularly such food as eggs and milk that was made hourly and with such careless and friendly obedience. Soon lorry-loads of eggs, milk, and butter would descend on London and the poor would come with jugs and baskets, and be sent on their ways rejoicing. Because by then, said Lavinia Reade catching an omnibus on the wing. By then, of course, I shall be rich.

Nevertheless she delayed this matter of wealth and munificence, to sit waiting for the truant Rollo to return and continue their pleasant life, and possibly his unfinished and unintelligible canvases. But Rollo did not return. Rollo was discovering that for an ambitious and penniless artist a mistress in the fifties with money is of more interest than one of twenty with no possessions beyond a seemingly inexhaustible capacity for enjoying all and every hour of the twenty-four. Rollo was in Venice with Mrs Saul Rennet, the enviably notorious Claudia Rennet, wife of the shipping magnate and mother of the lovely Rennet twins; leaving Miss Reade to grind her teeth when she remembered how often she had written: the beautiful Mrs Saul Rennet, the Famous Hostess, that well-known Patroness of the Arts; conscientiously adding those attributes of wealth: wit, fascination, and intellect.

How many times had she written of her as looking not a day older than her lovely daughters, when to the unprejudiced unjournalistic eye she was no other than an embalmed and painted old woman with a hunted look of having missed something, life or the latest lion or the morning massage, and could only buy for hard cash what others took by right of youth and love. Still, Rollo was now at the Palazzo Galli, on which its witty and lovely owner (the gossip-writers again) had recently spent more than £100,000, restoring and decorating. Singing for his supper like any of the sycophantic musicians and writers who gather, eager yet deferential vultures, around the carcases and dining-tables of the superlatively rich; except that Rollo sang at any hour; sang at a perpetual Royal Command, beginning possibly before breakfast.

And only a month since he had taken her to Paris on what seemed the last fifty pounds they would ever see. Fortunately she had not known that it was a farewell treat on the last of Rollo's honestly earned pence. And not a week after their return he was celebrating his good fortune (for it was extreme good fortune) with the ageing and exacting Claudia Rennet, adding with happy irony: And she is to give me my holidays on full pay!

Miss Reade could only cry out that he would need them if rumour was true, and that never again would he paint a picture worth painting. But that part of the prophecy could not have been right for Rollo had painted so many pictures that his name came glibly to the lips of lovely women who wished to hang on ancestral and Academy walls, looking as near an expensive fashion plate as they dared and yet with a flourish which gave to the paint a look of expense and permanence. Whereas four years later Miss Reade had got no further than sitting above a village on an afternoon in late July, thinking that nothing would show for another five months at least, and tossing her head on its long independent neck and saying aloud: I want her to be a gay young thing! I shall call her Bernardine.

But a cloud was passing across the sun. The brief spell of good weather, it meant, was about to break. One could see the first faint clouds of white dust whipped by the wind, far down across the plain beyond Schledstadt; where in the far distance the roads breathed a cloud of white dust before the storm. Even where she sat a small sudden wind, insidious agitator, was bending leaves and flowers in discontent.

Miss Reade stood up. She had an irresistible desire to walk to the top of the nearest hill and come suddenly on the sea. Possibly because one always expects to find the sea behind a hill. Behind a hill there can be only the sea. But she had not gone far when the loud and incessant chugging of the saw-mills stopped her. Ugly, inhuman sound. Everywhere the forests were being cut down. Already one could see the mutilated remains on some of the nearer hills, sudden shaved patches like a mange; a sick poodle, all worried. It hurt and dismayed her, the ruthless irreparable damage. Lavinia Reade turned away, as though she knew that she had no courage to face other people's stupidities; but only her own.

She was just in time as she came to the Marktplatz to see the little comedy of the War Memorial; an ugly granite cross enclosed in an iron railing, for which dreary growth the chestnut trees outside the Gemeinehüss had been cut down. Clumps of dahlias grew round it, pushing leaves and heads between the iron spikes. Obviously intent on catching one of the flowers, a little girl of some three or four years was walking slowly around the railing, humming. Miss Reade watched her with amusement; such a good-natured happy little thing, very busy. Suddenly, and as though the impulse was no longer to be resisted, the child reached out and picked a fat yellow dahlia, twice as large as the hand she stretched for it. At once and with a swift possessive fury the woman who was with the child gave her a resounding slap across the face and arm, tore the flower from her hand and threw it back inside the railing. The little thing cried on a long, dazed, hiccoughing note, as though something inside it had been torn. Its fat little legs gave way, and it sat down on the stones to a long bewildered sobbing.

Miss Reade ran across the Marktplatz, gathered the crying child high in her arms, and choosing the largest dahlia she could find, an intricate *rosace* of pink tongues, broke it off and put it between the child's fat tear-stained fingers. It stopped crying quite suddenly, and stared and stared.

—The flowers are for the dead, said the woman slowly and sententiously in German.

—No! said Lavinia Reade in her clear, intelligent voice. For the living! All things, said Lavinia Reade, showing her splendid teeth in a smile, all things are for the living. Only for the living.

She put the child down. In an agony of shyness, its nose buried in petals, it went straight to its mother's skirts and clung there. The woman, with her flat expressionless face turned aside, took the child's hand and they walked slowly away.

—Hello, interference! said an amiable and familiar voice. Now she will be soundly slapped and put to bed without her supper.

They watched the woman and child pass out of sight. Yes, Sebastian was right. The child would now be soundly slapped and put to bed without her supper.

—O women, women! cried Lavinia Reade passionately, as though she spoke of some malignant disease. She ached as though the shame had been hers. To strike a child for picking a flower larger than its own hand! No man could have been guilty of such unimaginative intolerance. Men made foolish mistakes; but not mean ones.

The hour was full of the sounds of home-coming; the grinding wheels of the ox-carts, the tired men trudging beside them, women with large white cloths knotted round their heads, children dangling thin legs and singing, all good-humouredly tired, all rather listless and emptied with fatigue from the day in the fields; all but the oxen with their eyes of onyx and ivory, and their effortless unhurried condescension.

Lorwich and Simeon Fenn coming from a side turning, crossed the Platz and climbed the steps Zum Goldenen Lamm. There was a strength about the squat Lorwich, an indefinable and pleasing reserve of energy; unhurried, ox-like. But the willowy Fenn looked pale and sullen, and as though the day's excursion had cost him a fortnight's energy.

Roused from her thoughts, Lavinia Reade sighed: To think that there are people with so few obstacles that they need climb mountains!

And after a pause she added slowly, and with unaccustomed bitterness: It does seem unfair that with the desires of women . . . they have not also the children.

(. . . the eunuchs of literature . . . the Vestalines of the grammar . . . the White Voices of free verse.

In a room bright as a witchball or the more crude forms of Venetian glass, Gabriel Bethemy receives his friends. Friends on the Bethemy principle that who is not for me is against me. Social and artistic London is pro-Bethemy or contra-Bethemy. Friends, therefore.

Each is glad to be here. It argues a certain distinction. Gabriel Bethemy does not choose at random. As offering each brings a little story, varying in wit but not in malice. To this, their social exchange and barter, they bring an aëry transient coinage: not even paper, just a little wind. And there is much washing of soiled linen at the literary fountains.

The room, that gaudy prettily self-conscious room, is filled with smoke and people, through which the lilt of tea-cup and glass has a fresh innocent sound of children laughing. The buffet groans under a load of inventive skill noticeably absent from the works of those who so liberally partake of it. Voices rise in mortal combat, rapier on rapier, fist to fist, attack, parry, thrust; to sink to earth, pause, rise again refreshed, uppercuts, body blows, clinchings, knock-out— One—Two—Three— Four—— The clock across the square strikes the hour. It is six o'clock on an evening in late April; an evening of blanched greys and vaporous blue which the trees in the neat Chelsea square turn (it is expected of them) to Whistlerian advantage.

The stage is set and two shall meet, though neither knows it, though as yet but one is in the room, and from the carved and gilded ceiling impatient Cupid, ribbon-girdled, wreathes in soft leaves his stubborn spear. One, wanderer but yesterday returned from foreign shores, hero of many an amorous combat, weary with a weight of reputation grown legendary and irksome, in whose hyacinthine beard Time's greying hand now seeks a resting-place. The other, a woman-virgin boy on whose untroubled brow the rosy light of youth, chaste locks of yellow gold in ardent disarray; one who, standing on the strand when the winds have soothed the seas (the mirrored semblance cannot lie!) surveys himself, and fears not Daphnis.

Lorwich lowering himself on to a chair groans: God! An antique! and poor Miss Fiffers at whom he stares in horror without seeing her, is never again quite sure, and to the end of life dares not finger the secret doubts of that thoughtless moment.

But Lorwich is referring to the chair whose tapered legs sway and creak at the burden so tactlessly imposed on them. He would get up, but dare not. He remembers that Gabriel Bethemy is very much the gentleman and therefore puts much of his soul and most of his pride in his furniture legs; and wishes that a gentleman's taste would occasionally run to something as decently solid as a tap-room bench. Lorwich, therefore, remains seated, hoping for the best. He is subdued and completely bored, and wonders how long it will be before some grinning and hospitable female will place a tea-cup in his hand, binding him more securely than Prometheus to his rock. It is eight years since Lorwich was last in England. He arrived from Paris but yesterday, and is already wondering where he will go tomorrow.

Meanwhile Gabriel Bethemy with grave, sleepy, impertinent face relaxed in welcome, picks, chooses, favours: like the sun, like a golden bee. He is speaking with that invisible but very audible silver spoon in his mouth. For some reason he avoids Lorwich, perched there helplessly on those legs more ridiculous than his own, and gazing fixedly at the wall where a blue Chirico stallion rears beside a pink-foaming sea. One can never be sure what Lorwich is thinking. He may be bored, and say so. He may use his sense of his fine theatrical presence to insist on his right as King of the assembled beasts.

As it happens Lorwich is thinking how splendidly Gabriel Bethemy and his brother Tressilian, maintain the English tradition of the gentleman. Gentlemen farmers, gentlemen trainers, gentlemen jockeys, gentlemen poets. And of how, by some inestimable dispensation of Providence, these two may sit astride life's fence; gentlemen among the artists: artists among the gentlemen. Rarely is a book of theirs published without it being remembered that an ancestor, one de Broy de Cuiy, came over with or after or before the Conqueror; and often they buy for sums not exceeding five guineas the works of struggling French and English painters, becoming with the minimum of effort and expense connoisseurs *and* patrons.

It gives Lorwich a definite malicious pleasure to observe how even Time has stayed his hour-glass for Gabriel who, the room being warm, is calling to his brother Tressilian: dear heart, would you open a window? Time stands still for Gabriel (Lorwich decides with feline insight) at an eternal thirty-three. What price had he paid, what bribe had he offered, to be allowed thus in the advance-guard of young moderns; though writing well before the War? And how rightly disdainful he looks; like some exquisite sheep perfumed for what slaughter? to be torn by what ridicule in the literary fangs of his enemies? to be . . . but a high playful voice is saying: *Well, well, well,* well! *and what are* you *doing* here! *And behold, high above Lorwich's chair now hangs the leaning tower of Alicia Prothero, whose novels are all they should be, and sell accordingly.*

Very gaunt and skittish and pencil-thin is Miss Prothero, holding aloft a champagne glass as a torch to light her wit and guide her footsteps in the ways of toothy charm. She is laughing now at Lorwich's plight, trapped on those spidery legs of undoubted worth but impoverished health; and Lorwich is laughing also (thank God, he has now an excuse not to move for the remainder of the evening) and dimly understanding why fundamentally he has never been able to appreciate women. An ungenerous thought, for this specimen (intellectually, at least) is above sample.

—*What what, what* what *are you writing now?* Miss Prothero asks. A repetition of words due to a studious technique of charm; girlish, light-hearted, irrepressible, irresistible. But Lorwich does not know this and thinks she has been drinking. He decides that he is writing a sequel to Lady Chatterley's Lover. He makes a sign. From afar Miss Prothero bends. He whispers the title in her ear. It is more than a little shocking; it is even disgusting. Miss Prothero shoots up again. Her cheeks are flushed. Her mouth is open. Her eyes are wide. She grimaces with excitement. So much so that Lorwich has almost the impression that she has this instant been raped, and has liked it. He leans back and watches this gaunt hollow campanile of a woman from the top of whom the thin sounds rock and jangle. From her height Miss Prothero is rapidly passing in review the various groups, choosing which shall be first recipient of her news; hesitates, falters, rallies, aghast and elated at such a word in her mouth, who till now has always sinned by proxy; and floats away heavy with the mystic burden of her secret.

Fragments of conversation detach themselves, are borne aloft, drift unclaimed, dying in wreaths of smoke, unmourned.

Some-one has just told Odo Quimpel (nervous as lightning and with the angular lines of a congolese mask) that Adrian Tims is not here as his wife is having a baby, and Odo is drawling: Now how did Adrian do that, d'you suppose? Breathe down her nostrils? A voice says quickly: O no. Adrian is a sadist. He probably poured hot tea down her back.

A large lady who has been dipped in flour and left unfried, is saying that all his virility (my dear) seems to have gone to his nose. And adds that, of course, he is fat. But that one expects of tenors; they spend so much of their time swallowing their words.

The thin little Jewess with the black ancestral curls on her shoulders is saying plaintively: But you forget, surely you forget?, there is a life below the stomach.

Once again Pirrie Ounce is complaining that his wife steals all his mistresses.

At the mention of wives Lorwich scowls mentally. His thoughts of Sidonie de Lagresin are hardly gracious; and certainly unfair. A wife has every right to enter the Casino and ask if her husband is still there, and on being told that Monsieur le Comte will be back but has left an hour ago, may add: alone?, and on hearing that a friend left with him, may decide to wait; may even wait one hour, two hours, three hours, motionless in shadow against a pillar, her mouth hard, her chin deep in the folds of her velvet cloak. There is a touch of frost in the air; one by one the lights go out; soon the street-cleaners will appear with their clatter of brooms and backchat; but such things do not trouble her static vigil and her eyes are fixed on the distance. At last a large yellow car turns in the drive and stops at the portico. It takes a certain time for the occupants to descend, but with much laughter and confusion they eventually do so. Le Comte Etienne de Lagresin comes first. Let alone walk he appears to find it difficult to stand, but with much good-humour and a little assistance he succeeds at last in staggering up the Casino steps. In his arms he carries a boy in the tightly buttoned scarlet of a page's uniform. The cherub's golden head lies sleepily against his shoulder, and as they pass through the lighted doors, the woman hidden in shadow hears a tired child-voice, half-sob: Mais non. Mais laisse-moi. Laisse-moi donc, cheri. A stout bearded man follows with another page tucked, like a bright little pig, under an arm. The child is very pale and has been sick all over the man's evening trousers. The chauffeur after handing out empty bottles to one of the Club servants, slams the car door, and drives off. The woman has not moved. Transfixed, frozen, she has let them pass. For nothing now avails Madame de Lagresin; nor her jewels, nor smoothly classic brow and tapering arms, nor the full-length pictures in those illustrated monthlies which set their worldly seal upon her beauty. On all these she may call; there is no answer. There is, however, influence; and three days later Lorwich leaves Paris. O all very politely, all very much as though it were a charming joke between man and man; but quite definitely leaves Paris. Who? How? *fumes Lorwich, perched on four expensive legs and horribly bored. Jealousy? Inadequate tips? Didi, le* groom *du Magenta? The de Lagresin chauffeur, under threat of dismissal?*

And then a voice that cuts like a sun through heavy cloud, dispelling with its rays his boredom and his anger. It is a languid voice, elongated, throaty, slurred, provocative. The voice is saying: Rome? But what is Rome but a beautiful and commodious water-closet surrounded by magnificent buildings?

The sentence does not by right of invention belong to Simeon Fenn, however well he uses it. He has overheard it not a month since, near the fountains of the Piazza di Spagna or coming down the steps of Santa Maria dei Monti, when the busy group of American tourists coming to a standstill, he was to hear the elderly bird-like little thing (from Polygon, O.) say shrilly: Waal, if you aarsk *me, it's one laang worrer-claset surrounded by just-too-luvverly buildings!* But his listeners cannot know this. Besides he has accented it almost beyond recognition, and also has had the good sense to see its possibilities. It goes well. The laughter is immediate.

Lorwich has turned. His gaze travels from the length and elegance of the speaker's leg to that fair starry face surveying the room as from its cloud. And all at once Lorwich is aware that he is carrying about with him an enormous stomach which floats when he walks, jellies when he laughs, sags when he sits. So humbling is love that he is on an instant and for the first time aware of his colossal and stunted frame: gross, uncouth, unworthy. But he has turned and gazes across his shoulder, his full eyes fixed and steady; and slowly, and as though willed, Simeon Fenn has turned and is looking at him. Sees, though his eyes do not move from the face, that heavy neck, that subtle perturbing varnish of dirt and brute force. As at a command Cytherea's rosy babe awakes, yawns, apprehends: takes aim. A moment and their wanton eyes (love's twin pools, the soul's fond mirror) are troubled. A blush is on youth's pale cheek. He lowers his eyes and is the first to turn away.)

Boum! Bou-bou-boum-boum. *Boum!* Heady martial sounds shattered the Sunday calm. A few mournful recruits sprang to attention, pranced about the cobbles, making solemn and spiritless clatter to an audience of delighted children and two barking dogs.

But Madame eyed the clock and snorted. Now the procession would be ruined. Bah! Les anti-clericaux!

Some-one reassured her. This, at its worst, could last but another twenty minutes, and the procession did not pass until four.

The military music crashed on: tuneless, discordant, insidious. Impossible to resist, impossible to think. At the door and out of the house before a man has realised what he is doing.

Sebastian was saying: To become a saint, my dear Lavinia, you need but transfer your erotic centre to your knees. Karl, noch ein viertel.

—As easy, said Miss Reade wearily, as easy as pinning one's colours to one's nose. No, thank you. No; no more for me.

No more wine (thought Lavinia Reade) and no more words. There was enough noise at the moment on the Marktplatz. Words and military music had much in common; both insidious and equally disturbing: the one to the ear, the one to the mind.

But Sebastian would talk. He was calling the American woman cold, angry, and ungrateful. He said she was her own punishment. He said the American woman was woman before she had been brought to her senses. Civilised woman, on the other hand, was woman made pleasant and palatable. The American woman was true woman: woman before she had been beaten into shape.

—But beautiful, said Lavinia Reade, half-heartedly.

Beauty? What on earth had beauty to do with it? Excrement was beauty to a fly! And Sebastian would have started once again on his theory that woman was made not for love but for pleasure, had not Miss Reade stood up and without ceremony walked to the window and stood staring.

After a while she said:

—Otto, your dog has no sex appeal. The other dogs avoid him.

—That is because he loves only me, grinned Otto.

—What a house! cried Miss Reade in mock alarm. What a house!

Meanwhile as an alternative to leaning over bridges by the hour and spitting at the water, the little blue soldiers leapt apart and back again, swung left and started off, swung right and were once more whence they started. Their discipline, French and individual, was disarmingly imperfect. It impressed the children. But the dogs seemed critical.

No more words (thought Lavinia Reade), no more words. At least not just now. Not on a Sunday afternoon. (How many times had Aunt Deborah used those cheerless words?) Could one not resuscitate or invent some god or hero to whom Sunday afternoon could be sacred in silence? And there fell a great calm upon the heart and ear of man, and the spirit of peace rested upon his habitation.

Standing there, staring from the window at the blue prancing soldiers, she felt a sudden, sharp, quivering movement. Once again, and it ceased. And she found it strange, and perhaps symbolic, that as she looked on at this clatter and mimicry of destruction, the new life she was to bear shuddered in the depths of her body.

Yet Sebastian had said that though biologically woman created, psychologically she could but destroy. Then men, one must assume, destroyed physically and created mentally, and the balance adjusts itself. Cold comfort this masquerade of war. Now even Sebastian's absurd prophecy had a disquieting threat of truth about it. For Sebastian held that men were becoming unnecessary, and must disappear. Indeed, the entire morning and that long road back from Engwiller now seemed to have been but a platform for Sebastian's theories and speculations.

They had been to the Ossuary. Fourteen thousand bodies had once packed it tightly to the ceiling (from some peasant war which the people spoke of as though it were yesterday); but the bones had crumbled until there was left only a heap of fragmentary dust, with here and there a skull and thigh and arm bone intact; big bones and large round skulls that still triumphantly proclaimed themselves the bones of strong men. (Looking at the skulls with their firm grinning teeth beautifully in place, she had thought: If I die now I shall look like this, and they will say: that one was young, look at those teeth! And it gave her a mournful pleasure to think of her teeth for ever whole and strongly clenched in death, as though the last word had been hers.) Above the Ossuary door was written:

WAS IHR SEID, SIND WIR GEWESEN.
WAS WIR SIND, WERDET IHR SEIN.

An official touch, misplaced, misunderstood, for the young dead are not sententious or vindictive. On the walls hung military buttons, caps, belts, and other oddments; left, the man in charge had told them, by the young men who went away to fight in the last war. Before they went they had come here to pray and light a candle, and those who returned had come again to hang these offerings on the walls. And that had troubled her more than the pile of young bones, the thought of the young coming to pray to the young, who also, some three hundred years since, had marched away from these villages.

But Sebastian was indifferent. He said that the last war was probably the end of man in more ways than one. The modern woman with her militant sterility could quite easily run the world on her own. He said the female was now active and in the ascendant, while to-day the function of the male was limited. For the mere continuance of the race man could be reduced to the male sexual organ. The world was changing too radically and the male virtues were no longer needed. War was not a need; it would become obsolete and the soldier would disappear. Manpower was not a need, soon all would be calculated by mechanical horse-power. Courage, enterprise, foresight, endurance were useless in a modernly organised community. Therefore all the qualities which made man supreme fell away. The men grew effeminate. Their services were not required. Only the women (said Sebastian) remained women. Their new activity and independence (a lack of servility) was mistaken for masculinity, but was merely adaptation. Already the more civilised (industrialised) a community, the more easily were the men dispensed with. A natural process. Where not so long ago it needed a man to guide a horse, to-day you had a woman guiding from 40 to 4000 horse-power. The more mechanical a community, the more feminine: as America, Russia, England. Only in natural (peasant) communities, such as Italy, Spain, the Balkans, France, the man still retained his power. To fight Nature it still required a man. To fight with machines, woman sufficed.

Sebastian said that the fact that a man always puts up a better performance than a woman did not matter at all. It did not make him indispensable. Small degrees of efficiency did not count. Man was no longer necessary when his job could be done almost as well by a woman and a machine. And as soon as he was no longer indispensable he ceased to exist. Only the indispensable is needed and created. That is Nature's demand and supply. In time all that would be required of man was the male semen.

As a living example of how well this worked there were the Ceratoids, most grotesque and efficient of all living creatures, the oceanic angler-fishes, who are all female, the male being dwarfed and parasitic on the females. One might say that here at last the female has found the perpetual male. And he told her how these female fish, solitary, sluggish, floating about in the darkness of the middle depths of the ocean, had at first found it difficult to find a mate, until this difficulty was overcome by the males themselves, who, as soon as they were hatched, and when they were relatively numerous, sought the females and if they found one held on to her and remained attached for life. They first held on by the mouth, but in time the lips and tongue fused with the skin of the female and the two became completely united. This mouth is toothless and closed in front and he is unable to feed himself, so he is fed by the blood of the female, for the blood streams are now continuous. And she now has an infinitesimal male permanently attached to the top of her head between the eyes, or under the body below the jaws. The Ceratoids were unique among back-boned animals in having dwarfed males of this kind, and unlike all other animals in having males fed in such a manner by the females. But that was only a matter of time, said Sebastian. The idea was too sound for Nature's humour and requirements to overlook. The trouble saved would be incalculable. And how much more pleasant a world, with women no longer dissatisfied and masters of the situation, and the harassed male no longer compelled to work for them.

All of which had been less real than the sight of a field of cabbages so exultantly blue that it had seemed to reflect the sky.

—Not merely blue blood, had said Lavinia Reade ironically, but the authentic purple.

Yet the rash prophecy of the perpetual and parasitic male which had not concerned her at all this morning, had now become less amusing. For no words, however plausible, could weigh against that tender and despairing grip that had clutched her a moment since, while the mimic soldiers pranced and Sebastian's cynical words made ugly echo among these simple unalterable things. Such as the old woman at the window opposite jumping a child above the flower-pots so that it might see what all that noise meant in the square. The old woman was taking the child most seriously and pointing out dogs, and the stork nest, and possibly several small members of the family gaping in the square; explaining how brave and significant it all was, quite as though the whole world was but a background for this latest arrival on it. (But in a village a baby *is* the very latest news, thought Lavinia Reade.)

Simple things, she thought. Simple, unalterable things. There was the woman with the tiny child in the scarlet boots, who came each evening to the inn corner to meet her husband home from work. When he appeared far down the street she would hold the child high for them to catch a first sight of each other, and then start running. Such a swift, lovely, unalterable impulse, the woman's holding-up of the child to its father home from work. And when she had remarked on the profusion of walnuts on the trees lining the roads, she had been told: Ah, a good year for nuts means that many women are pregnant! That, too, was a lovely eternal thing, linking their women so warmly, so unquestioningly, with the earth, sharing the effortless burden of trees and fields.

How pleasant, here among these people. Why could one not live here always? This village was big enough. This was a world. A woman's world: world without end. Why go back? To what? To words? To the hermaphroditism of modern woman in a modern world? To that bright protective-colouring of good fellowship that is life in a great city? From a long dissembled frustration to the dissatisfactions of old age? Must she, too, capitulate? Of all ugly decaying things, a woman dissatisfied. How wearying it was, that modern indecency: the frustrated woman. And how futile, seeing that nothing could be done about it. A woman's dissatisfaction led nowhere. Women should be pleasant peaceful creatures, generous in youth and wise in age. What more could one ask of them? What more could they ask? Men might be restless, because men could achieve. But women achieve mostly a half-achievement, and at best nothing that a man cannot better. Except the holding-up of a child with scarlet boots to see its father in the distance; or explaining with extreme seriousness to a doll-face peering over the geranium pots, as though nothing was so important in all the world as the proper understanding between grandmother and her very latest grandchild. Perhaps if Aunt Deborah had not been so strict, so coldly hostile, and she had not run away and had never written that absurd napoleonic letter: when I am famous I shall return! (Whenever she saw black earth she thought of Norfolk and of how in winter the powdery frost sits on it like sugar on plum-pudding and the windmills are like old men or witches with faggots on their backs, and sometimes on Sunday afternoons when one has been more than usually severely punished like a Cross being lifted once again.)

Here in this changeless setting, in some angular house, a husband with few words, whom one would help in his fields, a table-full of children, one's own wine in the cellars, one's food stored for the winter, and washing-days and baking bread, and never again to say a bright or witty thing, and to become old without noticing it, having no regrets. Here where it was a matter of man and beast: food and shelter. For they were shelters, not houses, either for their animals or themselves, or for the storing of food. And all the sounds were animal sounds. Hens and children. Swallow calling swallow. And man preparing for winter as for a siege.

A voice cried excitedly: Here they come!

For the soldiers were gone, faces were at the windows, people were looking over her shoulders, and beside her Otto in his black Sunday clothes was leaning on the sill.

First the children in white and pale blue innocence, supplying with short steps and high astringent voices the pace and rhythm to which the procession moved; and then the priest whose lean face wasted its subtlety on the village air (a disappointed man, thought Lavinia Reade); and then several handsome young novices from the seminary, a few sisters of mercy, pale gulls with spread wings, planeing behind them. Several saints, male and female, swayed howdah-wise above the procession, but which exactly on this particular day had risen and gone to Heaven was a difficult choice. The men were painted plaster, but the women were gracious in gaudy skirts stiff with tinsel, the large lumps of glass jewellery on their crowns and breasts glinting prettily in the light and distracting from the enormous bunches of grapes with which they were hung. For grapes were everywhere: the real reason and the best one. Hung over Saint Sebastian's arrows and round the women's hands and throats, threaded through Saint Joseph's halo and over Saint Anthony's outstretched arms; everywhere wreaths of white and purple grapes in a profusion of leaf and tendril. Re-enthroned Bacchus moved in sober measure to the Agnus Dei. Now came the girls who left the village each morning for the Schledstadt factories, very self-conscious and very condescending in their silk stockings, their high-heeled shoes, their rouged lips. (Another generation and we'll have millions more tin cans and no children, said a voice.) And lastly the old women, clutching long candles in tenacious yellowed claws. Miss Reade who had seen them at work in the vineyards was surprised. Why are they the last? she wanted to know. Without them there would be no grapes!

Some-one pointed proudly to Karl's grandmother, an astonishingly robust and monumental old lady carrying a heavy banner as readily as though it were an umbrella.

—Your grandmother certainly is a remarkable woman, Sebastian said to Karl.

—She is silent, said the youth indifferently. An excellent thing in grandmothers.

Miss Reade looked on without pleasure. The town-crier and his little drum was a more amusing sight, yet it brought scarcely one head to a window. Besides it was such a joyless slow-moving thing, out of harmony with its true purpose and reduced to the measure of a few subdued children chanting in questionable Latin. And Sunday, as usual, seemed to have fallen on them like a blight, leaving them ill at ease and incredibly mediocre. How drearily people misunderstood their purpose and the harmony of a setting! These should be flushed with love and wine and rosy-cheeked children. How willingly people denied themselves; and what a constant betrayal they were, friends or strangers, however little one asked of them; by their stupidity or by their meanness, or an unawareness, or an indifference. They failed. They fell short. They cheated. In the kingdom of the blind the one-eyed may be king, thought Lavinia Reade. The two-eyed is outcast.

Otto seeing the look on her face, misconstrued it. Some-one must have told her the man was gone. Or had she guessed?

Women had an instinct for such things. And she was sad and unusually pale. Otto had a romantic eye; he would have been surprised to learn, among other things, that Miss Reade was no longer nineteen. He admired her. She gave him an impression of good-humour and courage. And there was no French mincing nonsense about her; no airs; no paint and powder; no pin-point heels. A companion for any man, thought Otto. And of how many women could a man say that? And Otto felt a sudden anger against the fool who, for a moment and as he left, had seemed to clutch at his hand like a drowning man. Enjoying himself now, thought Otto. Ingrate. Deserter. And where could he find such another? Not where he was looking now, thought Otto. He'd soon find his mistake. And serve him right if it was too late.

Thoughts which would have surprised Harrion who, tired of watching the liquefaction of the Strasbourg houses in the oily surface of the canal, had at last found a bench in a park, and was sitting there lost in the contemplation of an ornamental flower-bed.

He must have been hungry, for he could think of nothing but hors-d'œuvre.

O men were gay and filled with a bright nonsense! They saw things as children saw them: for the first time; where women saw them with the old old eyes of women, nothing escaping them. It was as though men were born with new eyes, and women with women's eyes.

Particularly at this hour the Wynstub was loud with masculine good-humour, drink, argument, and laughter. Not what was said, nor how wise, nor how foolish, but a zest that gave to the hour its charm and emphasis. Here and thus men had argued, laughed, drunk the centuries away; and would again. Inevitably at this evening hour it would be alive with such sounds; the same arguments would break, the same complaints be made, the same conclusions reached; as serious, as ribald, and as ephemeral.

It had the mellowness (she thought) of the Dutch still-life hung, ever-crooked, above the door. An advertisement, a cheap German oleograph used by a local poultry merchant; but no oleograph however cheap could make vulgar the Dutch school. Perhaps because their values were true; fruit, game, people grouped about their tables, above their music. They had their conventions. No Fra Angelico saint was more frail than the transparent asparagus bundles of these incomparable food and flower painters. A glass half-filled or overturned; a few nuts broken in the foreground; a fly; a lady-bird; a lemon trailing a luminous curl. For drama: the fish's eye.

Caught in the swirl of sound, Miss Reade was marvelling at how good men were, how unself-conscious; how gay and how nonsensical. (A fly falls in some beer and one of them drinks it, or to every one's dismay sees it in time!, and all the business of cards and argument is held-up for the laughter to stop, and stop only to break again louder and merrier than before.) Women: why could they not laugh? Why was the divine male gift of nonsense denied them? Why had men alone this gift of effortless gaiety? Did Eve bite it off with the apple, that vague female resentment as though life must be always pleasant, made of an elegant, fadeless, rosy texture; and that sense of brooding responsibility, that censorious outlook, that small intolerance? Man laughed (Lavinia Reade was thinking) without effort or after-thought; yet man worked, worked and saved and cared for and fed wife and children, fought, invented, rolled the earth along somehow on his back, and was always ready to laugh at nothing; particularly at a fly dropped in a mug of beer and all but swallowed.

—And after that what do we do when we want to honour a man? We put a chain round his neck and call him a watchdog of the city! (A dig this at some local councillor who drank only at l'Agneau Noir.)

To which the owner of the superb red mushroom of a nose, prime cellar-grown under the barrel, said: And where's the difference between them, anyway, except that one lifts an elbow at every corner and the other a leg?

At intervals the group of young Germans on a walking tour broke into song, in that lush German voice of a man who has eaten and drunk well, and sings to thank for it. They were noticeably German with their rounded buttocks, handsome blond faces, and pink moist lips.

Now Lorwich was talking on wine countries and their supremacy in Art, and proving that the picturesque is a remnant of barbarism.

A voice (Otto, she thought half-turning) boomed: . . . a case of do not touch my goods. But stealing itself is not immoral. It is only that it affects the man who had the money and now has it no longer!

An uproar, a thunderclap of protest and agreement. A glance risked at Madame. But Madame was laughing; perched on the black horsehair sofa so curiously like herself, her soul's sister. Madame is in extreme good-humour; for the verdict is not till next week; the trial is again postponed, and her importance is no longer momentary but cumulative.

The large man with the beret pulled down so tightly that it seemed to have hit him on the head, was saying that you can give them the freshest eggs and still they will make the heaviest omelettes. A matter of climate. No wonder they left their own country and were to be found the world over! What other people had ever been so eager to leave their own part of the earth? When the English boasted themselves world colonisers and victors, they should remember their climate and be more humble. A cold selfish people. The climate again. No endearment except for the dog. No sugar except for the horse. And a people utterly without religion. Had they ever seen an English clergyman? The bony sort with large teeth and long noses and reedy necks wriggling in a large collar? But it was unbelievable! It was something made for Christmas to amuse the children.

Sebastian was beating on the table as though thumping himself on the back. He was insisting that genteel people work more than the honest worker, only they produce nothing. Hence genteel discontent and the worker's hearty disposition. Whilst the simple person (the worker, the peasant) is positive, he finds joy only in positive things: a good feed, a good drink, a good laugh. The genteel person finds joy only in genteel pleasures: a little snicker, a little bitter word, a little criticism of appearances: in fact, in purely negative non-existent things. A hearty man understands a solid hefty female: he gets, so to speak, a good meal out of her. The genteel male will find his pleasure in parading some feathers and paint and does not ask for a woman to be there at all.

—The fascination of glass is the fascination of the eye.... Take this dark green-black bottle. A pool of water has an hypnotic effect. In an open space, a light in the distance is eerie, haunting. And the moon, the sycophantic moon staring a man in the face.... Instinct then has always been a finer instrument than science. Much that science has dismissed she has had to re-admit. If telepathy exists it means there is a human receiving and broadcasting set. One (that of science) was invented yesterday. One is eternal. We may dismiss such things as phantasy. But our mechanical receiving and broadcasting set is primitive and unfinished compared with telepathy. In other words, Science is coarse and full of errors where Nature is subtle and infallible. To come to the ridiculous: you say to a peasant (an illiterate): there is a machine and you put a pig in at one end and it comes out a sausage at the other. He laughs. He laughs at mechanical science: you are affronted and amazed at his stupidity. But when he says to you: I was in a field and I felt that something was wrong and I had to stop work and ran home to find that the horse had kicked my little son and killed or injured him, you (the scientist) laugh. That is the coarse and imperfect (mechanical) laughing at the infallible and subtle. Saying peasant means, of course, a man nearer to Nature than the scientist. If we knew more, we should probably know why Nature gives us this instinct of fear for the unknown. Possibly to preserve us. To prevent us falling into a trap or facing a danger. For all we know, whatever is mystery may be Nature's self-preservation for man....

One of the young Germans, angry at the new red-brick fire-station stark in its utilitarian rawness in the street behind the Gemeinehüss, was saying: They keep history so sacred in a book and obliterate it in life. They give away the original and keep a description of it.

Madame said impatiently: But, of course, your history books will put out our fires.

Everyone laughed; no doubt excessively to propitiate Bellona, who acknowledged the tribute by polishing the rim of a glass with contentious vigour. For a fraction of a second her glance intercepted that of the English Mees. He is gone! said Madame's bright malicious eye. He is gone!

Let him go! cried Lavinia Reade's quickened pulse. Let him go! And good-bye to all regrets and yesterday's mistakes. For now she knew that she would always be as foolish as she was now, even when she was quite an old woman. For always she would be in the midst of life and feeling. She was not one of life's spectators, but its ardent participant. How then regret mistakes, when one could but repeat and repeat them? She who lived too intensely to see herself as the centre of the situation until it was too late, or long past. But never again would she be ashamed when she laughed or cried or found things more than she could bear, only to forget them a month hence. She knew that this must always be, for hers was the secret of the artist: intensity. Where there was no intensity there was no enthusiasm, and where there was no enthusiasm there was deadness and decay. And to be without emotion was to be old. For the old are without emotion. It hardens like their arteries, and is politely called being wise. But intensity was youth. And not merely youth but eternal youth. It might be frowned on. It might not be fashionable. It might not be correct: but it was right. For intensity was life. And life she had abundantly. She was not fortunate in her love affairs. She gave before being asked, and again when they had ceased asking. She was the type of woman who runs calling through the street: Gilbert! Gilbert! And to the very end, if there was any giving to be done, she would be the one who gave. But never mind. Some women had security; security of affection, security of possessions. But security was not for her. Only when she was tired, disappointed, sick or fearful of old age, did she long for this security and unimaginativeness of other women. But were it offered she would not accept it. For she took life as men take it: as it came. And all that it had taught her could be summed-up in: now. Now. Not yesterday nor to-morrow: but now. This hour. This moment. This was all. This the answer to every question: *now*. Later one was swept aside like a floor that is tidied, new sand is sprinkled like earth on one's grave and others sit and drink and argue. But there is Now. And that was the sum-total of all happiness. That was the secret of intensity, of life, of eternal youth. And she thought of the many people she knew, interesting enough people, drifting in far-away London as in the middle depths of an ocean, and all of them neither happy nor unhappy, but only distracted. And she thought that whatever else she lost in life, never must she lose this sense of living for the moment, and of denying that moment nothing: for what was each hour but a gift that brought one nearer death?

Miss Reade shook back her head, an unconsciously arrogant

movement, as though to hold it high, high above all other heads; and Sebastian happening to look up just then was reminded of Maurice Barrès: J'aime la femme un peu folle: l'inspirée.

But he did not mention it, being occupied with an exquisitely sensitive drunken song:

Ah, ciel! quelle ivresse!
Quatre seins et quatre fesses....

—No, no, no. A matter of climate. Catholicism and wine. Protestantism and beer. And if you wanted a practical working religion then Catholicism was the more amenable of the two, for it had the only pagan rites left. Its devotees might lose anything from their virginity to a buttonhook and there was always someone to complain to about it.

—And did God model or carve when he was making the English? And did he blow into them a soul or just a little wind? And why did this most carnivorous of nations have its teeth set like rabbits?

—But in a village the burden is shared equally, each man and woman contributing. In the city father is a little clerk and all the family lives on his back.

—Destroy a human being in five seconds and it is a crime. Destroy him in thirty years and it is right and natural. What do you see when you go for a walk? Church—fort—castle, castle—fort—church, surrounding each village. Wherever human beings are gathered there you found the castle and fort to milk them. Christ said Feed them. The Church misunderstood and sheared them.

But Lorwich seemed to think it was being taken altogether too seriously. Probably it was all an advertisement for the Jewish genius for being born in a manger and ending in the bank manager's chair.

Whereupon Sebastian (doubtless wishing he had thought of it himself) raised a heavy head and called out: Maestro Rafaello, non te n'incaricar!

—Perspiration for the many, my dear friend. Perspiration for the many and inspiration for the few.

—What a waste it was! What a waste! And it will come again. Not in my day, but you, young woman, you will see it.... (The old man nods and nods as though this makes his prophecy unassailable. He is telling Miss Reade about the War, in which he lost two sons. He is very old and brittle, and as though held together secretly by wire and string, as old people so often seem. The marionette made man.) All the vines were ruined. What could one expect with only women and children in the fields and vineyards, and the artillery commanding the mountains. No, his sons were not killed in France. In Poland. POLAND. Ya, Poland. Poland was an awful place, it seemed. Poor, hungry, filthy. The people live like pigs. All in rags and on a crust of bread. It was a shock to the Alsatian troops, used to a good table and warm beds and plenty in the cellars. They hated Poland and the stupid superstitious Poles. Only the churches were rich and filled with gold, and jewels sewn all over the statues of their saints. But my sons said our pigs lived warmer! Then why were they sent to Poland? Herrje, because you had to send them as far away as you could or they'd come home again: and rightly, too, with the corn and wine all spoiling and nothing but women and children scurrying about like frightened hens, and the soldiers trampling everything and always drunk and threatening civilians. That's why they were in Poland. They sent the Paris troops to Africa, the southern troops to the north, the northerns south or overseas, and our boys to Poland. Because you can shoot deserters by the handful but not by the battalion. That was one of the gravest problems of the War, especially for France and Belgium. It takes a great deal more than patriotism for a boy who has been brought up on the land to see the corn trampled. They don't mind fighting in the towns, that's all right, that's all towns are for because towns don't count. But it hurts them most in the fields....

I should have been called Pandora! she thought; full of hope again. Not that she knew that it was hope. She knew only that she was alive and at peace with herself once more. Even this old man with his prophecy of War could not frighten her now. Not even a prophetic glimpse of the folly of men in a world without vision, world in which she must live, the old had made it, the young must accept it, and all who came after must accept what they found here. It didn't matter! One was alive. Only the moment mattered, now and always. Once again she felt that exhilaration of the blood when one is so aware of being alive that one could die and not know it until long afterwards. And that, of course, meant the return of hope. For hope attacks, where possession can only defend. (Which may be why few rich people are really happy, thought Lavinia Reade.) So that hope creates energy and energy creates life. Against evidence, against experience, still hope does not give up. Because, of course, everything had disappointed (did one sit down to think of it), beginning with the nightingale. How angry, how cheated she had felt, waiting, waiting, sitting on the windowsill, her knees drawn up to her chin, her toes tucked in her long flannel nightdress, waiting for the first fluted notes of *La donna è mobile* to come trilling above the woods. What, was that all? But a blackbird was prettier! Was it for this that one had pinched oneself awake until the whole house slept? With their: sings like a nightingale! What *could* one expect from a nightingale but to sing like an operatic tenor? And not even a ballad. And everything was a little like that. But in the end one emerged. One discarded Make Believe at last for the happiness of being alive. Reality transcended the illusory, and this was life's reward, the having of one's finger-tips tingling with a certain drunkenness in merely being alive, and being enclosed, as now, in a drowsy warmth of friendly voices.

This exhilaration of life was her gift, though she had never understood it before, to those she met or had loved. But only Rollo had known. Rollo loving both God and Mammon, and deciding that though God might be necessary Mammon was indispensable. M'Hugh was not among those who mattered either to God or Mammon. Harrion had known it, and because of something secret and confused, had for a time extinguished it. But not for long.

—I should have been called Pandora! thought Lavinia Reade, and would have liked to lean her head out of the window and get it soaked in rain. For outside the rain was bearing down on the stones as though to crush them. It had begun an hour ago, the first drops ringing on the ground like large pennies, and then a summer storm had set in, whipping up the air, gathering up the winds, washing everything clean, washing everything away, making things fresh and new again. Rain was an eager thing.

(But Harrion, who loathed it, lay on the bed in a fitful doze. The miauling of a child came to him through an open window. The roof drip-dripped. On, on and on, the sounds of water flowing. It was as though the ceaseless battering was a deluge threatening to bear him down; he put out a hand and clutched the edge of the bed. The rain poured on. Through it all the crying child hiccoughed meaningless things.)

. . . and so you think he has the right to appeal to the rest of the world to interfere in the Russian religious persecutions? And it is not political, no? No! Very well. But when in 1922 the Turks were massacring the Armenians and a deputy of Armenian refugees begged the Pope to help them . . . I know, dear children. I suffer. I am praying for you. And they were gently pushed on to Cardinal Gasparri. We know, dear children. We suffer. We are praying for you. Yes, says the deputation, but can you not make some public gesture? Cannot our cause be put before the world? Cannot prayers be said in every Catholic Church throughout the world for the souls of our poor martyrs? Ah that . . . *that*, no! For that we have no power, dear children....

—What's that? said Sebastian, suddenly alert.

It was repeated, vehemently. The Pope interfering in Russia's affairs and appealing to the world. But when the Turks were massacring the Armenians . . .

—When the *what*?

The narrator was losing patience. When the Turks were massacring the Armenians . . .

Sebastian groaned. Good God! Haven't they caught Michael Arlen *yet*?

Some-one suggested that the Book of Revelation was the work of a man in the last stages of D.T.'s. Didn't he first see two candelabra, and the next time he looked they were six, and then they were nine.... If the Bible survived it would be thanks to sailors!

Lapped by the warmth and friendly flow of voices, Miss Reade smiled upon the room. The young German student, who throughout the evening had been trying unsuccessfully to attract her attention, responded eagerly. But her smile was unseeing, impartial. It rested awhile on Simeon Fenn, languidly suffering this plebeian hour for love's sake; and she wondered again (as she never ceased to wonder) wherein his vaunted attraction lay, and decided finally that the fact that Lorwich had need of him temporarily justified his existence. And thought how each and every vice was acceptable, except meanness: for meanness alone of them all could not be explained by an excess of emotion or pleasure. It was the one vice that was not a misdirection of energy or generosity.

 . . . till we come to *l'obolo di San Pietro*. Only the Pope could have found the way to exploit both worlds so neatly by making earth and heaven work for him. What a super rag-and-bone shop they had started in Rome! Pieces of rag and bits of bone hawked down the ages by super-ragmen....

Whereupon Lorwich urging that one God was ample for the shopkeeper though inadequate to the creative artist, and (as an impartial observer) stressing the dour provincialism of the Protestant sects, struck the final and victorious blow for Catholicism by leaning across the table and saying quietly: Tell me. Which would you rather: dine with the Borgias or take tea with Dean Inge?

Strasbourg is a diversion of the Comic Muse; a work of the Foolish Virgins. Unserious, cross-stitched houses appear to have been playing leap-frog and to have been caught in the act. One looks up, they steady themselves. Their smile is Voltairian. The swaying argus-eyed roofs stare, wink, hiccough. At no hour are they quite sober.

Yet the effect is deliberate; nothing has been left to chance. All is composed as a flower-piece, the whole linnet-coloured with care and tenderness. The river moves thickly, the crude oil surface unhurried, and at its edge the houses in full sail anchor a moment. After the night's storm the air is fresh and pleasing, and the activity everywhere is Monday's rebuke to Sunday's idleness. In the wash-houses the women kneel in their boxes of straw, scrubbing with large brushes, thrusting out their arms from time to time to swish the linen in the oily waters. Clothes baskets litter everything, and cats, and children. Above towers the Cathedral's single spire, that mighty amphora raised to heaven. The bells begin a deep, slow, reverberation; now a warning, now a command. In such a voice God spoke to Adam, to Michelangelo.

Harrion stood up. The young woman with the child in her arms, who had shared the bench, watched him from sight, wondering why she should be filled with pity for him. She was pale and sickly looking, as though the child had been wrenched from her leaving her bloodless and transparent.

Unmistakably the produce of a picturesque old town, he was thinking. In small dark rooms, pale, ill children, ugliness and ill-health on all their faces; bad teeth, unhealthy skins. (An epidemic of infantile paralysis was spreading alarmingly just then in the Bas Rhin, but one did not need to wait on the newspapers for the information.) The more narrow and picturesque the street, the sicklier seemed the children. The people themselves were white-faced, unindividual, hard-working, *abbruti;* with ill-fitting clothes of mediocre colour. Faces matched houses, stubbornly out of square. But in their physical disability lay their architectural advantage, as by their faces one saw how it came that they could no more have built symmetrically than the Italians could have built asymmetrically.

Little blue soldiers bobbed about, their humorous alert French faces in immediate contrast. But blue was the wrong colour. Blue became an eyesore. Everywhere the French had put up their hard, Parisian-blue plaques and taken away the German script, so that the houses were no longer written across, their names clinging like tendrils to a vine, and spread to the grateful eye as a page from Gutenberg's own Bible. Everywhere the beautiful wrought-ironwork had been taken down, lost or shut away in museums, and replaced by bits of white and blue enamelled tin.

Suddenly between the streets the Cathedral hangs like some precious tapestry that has caught fire in a thousand places. High above the world in an ecstasy of their own the bells plunge and crash, as though hammering at the door of heaven itself. But the Cathedral square was thronged with people. He hesitated. But something of immediate importance seemed about to happen, and before he could retreat the crowd had grown larger. He was shut in by a troupe of boy-scouts whose willing knees seemed (as usual) frail for such an exaggeration of cooking array and rucksack; and by eager voluble Americans with their strange insensitive children.

Standing directly beneath it, the Cathedral had the glow of rusty ironwork. The treatment of the stone is the treatment of wrought-iron, as involved, as wayward. Here has been done with stone what the Chinese did with ivory; air has been let in, a third dimension added. At intervals blue doves rose and scattered, exchanging scrolls for apostolic beards, cherub heads for saintly wrists.

But the crowd was moving, and the effect was hypnotic. Many brave men have done many brave deeds, but among them has not as yet been the moving backward through a mass of advancing crowd. So that it was only when he was inside, wedged at the back against a wall, that he found he was in the side chapel, given-up to the worship of its famed astronomical Clock. But going out now was too great an effort, even had it been possible. The attendants were fussy and irritable enough, with their brusque little rudenesses and their Silence là-bas! Silence! There was too much light, though the doors were now closed. It came in broad shafts from windows behind the altar, through stiff staring apostles, bright blue, bright red, bright green; new as a pack of unshuffled cards. How misunderstood, these modern efforts at stained glass. The colours are crude, the pieces of glass are large, where the colours should not only be sober in the extreme, but the pieces of glass minute and held together by lead-work in such a way that there is more lead than either glass or colour. The modern effect becomes that of a bar-parlour by daylight, when it should be that of a forest at sunset. He turned gratefully to a small rose-window glowing like jewelled earth, and remembered that traveller's tale of the old craftsmen using the blood of traitors for the sombreness of their reds. But the blood of innocent men would scarcely have been too high a price for such perfection. And he thought how the impermanence of to-day was not the result of war or the decline in religious belief, though that counted, but was due to the impermanence of the goods of life; the manufactured goods, the plethora of religious beliefs; and the impermanence of these goods is responsible for the sense of impermanence in spiritual matters. When men built this they knew that it was for ever. They built their homes for ever, their beliefs for ever, and, in some unfathomable way, their literature and their arts for ever. We build for to-day, we live for to-day, we think for to-day, we die to-day.

But the *Silence!* and the sh-shings were growing louder. It needed but a minute to the hour for the little figures in the mechanical clock to do their turn, bob out, be blessed, all except Judas, when the Cock must crow and flap his wings; and then everyone would breathe a sigh of awed relief (as though wireless, cinema, refrigerators, telephones, wrist-watches, and other hourly instances of ingenious mechanism were unknown) and push back again into the street.

Yet to have seen one thing is to have seen all things. A grain of sand and all shores, an incoming tide and the farthest ocean. A certain number of words, and nothing is left to say. If this was all and afterwards there was nothing: then this was not enough. And if there were other worlds, then this was but a waste of time. Christ's remark about gaining the world and losing one's soul was so good as to be unnecessary. For who has lost his soul has lost his world. Once attained the solitudes are too bleak. The urges, good or ill, of one's fellow-men are no longer impressive. Life's most urgent function remains that of defecation, and man's most pressing need washes down to the rivers (however weary or not these may be). The rest is a lid to cover putrefaction; a warding-off of the inevitable nothing. The earth contracts to a few square feet, seeing that it is bounded individually by man, and man is sewer-bound. (Which may partly explain why the naïveté of a Jean-Jacques Rousseau can undermine the godhead of a Voltaire. And not only can, but invariably does.)

It was then, just as the first stroke summoned the first apostle, that Harrion looked up. But it was not at the Clock, with the others, that he looked. He was seeing for the first time that column rising like smoke, umbilical cord binding earth and heaven, revealing itself slowly without visible beginning and end; and understanding how it came that he rose at the sound of the bells as though summoned.

If the window was blood then this was bone, for whatever is austere and sepulchral in the Gothic was here in this fluted column carved from the very bones of acolytes, from the emaciated ribs of saints. And there suspended, leaning a little forward, her lips to the swirl of trumpet along whose length her Gothic fingers rested, her wings in shadow, brave, outward-looking, poised for stony flight, she looked down at him. Up, up, up the fluted column in ascension perpetual: calm, other, sexless. It is looking up that makes one giddy, and leaves one dazed, cutting off reason in the pushing back of the head. Such the messenger, such the message. And it is for him, for he alone had looked up and answered it. All sick things must be thrust aside. All that is tired and sick, he thought, is human garbage. It seemed to him then that she smiled. It was not impartial. It was the bringing of a message and to those who understood it, she smiled. Now it was a matter of days or hours, yet when the moment came to him (he felt) she would know.

Yet it was an ugly thing, seen face to face. Not death itself, but that which came after; those about one, all the unpleasantness of disposing of a dead thing, the putting of it in a box and the wheeling of it away, and the digging of the fewest possible inches of earth in which to hide it. For now he saw, accepting as he did the decision, that the horror of death lay in what they did to one afterwards, when there was no redress, no restraint, no privacy. And he shrank from the sudden realisation that soon he, who recoiled from contact with his fellowmen, who all his life had feared the crowd, he, who with difficulty had taken another's hand in his own, would lie packed among the crowd in death, shoulder to shoulder, depth to depth, powerless, indiscriminate, uncaring. Then not in the loneliness of the grave lay its horror, but in its promiscuity. Then not even in death was one alone. Yet she smiled. Suspended in an ecstasy of stone in ascension perpetual, lifted above man and his tumult, one looked down and one smiled. Granted that, one would smile. At last one could smile if one might lean thus in endless half-light from a piece of tessellated stone; or swing in the light of day from a dizzy height looking downward with sightless eyes; or standing on a shaft of filigree point a hand to lure a pigeon, and rest seven hundred years.

The rainbow struck the earth in a shaft of light: the javelin Saul threw in anger. A bowl of light has been shaken and cracked and the pieces float, pause, drift, and sink, leaving on the sky the justification of the soul's folly, the damnation of common sense, all the miracles of the Middle Ages, all mysticism, all mystification. Cities of the plain, ascensions, annunciations, fiery chariot trails, rays whose swords pierce infidel and martyr, blue holes ripped in the grey through which chant the heavenly hosts, and in the distance the hills where God walked with his prophets.

—It was worth the bites, said Miss Reade at last, slapping her bare arms.

But Ittswiller was still a mile away. And at the thought of turning away from it all, from the great length of plain spread at her feet (for that pencil *was* the Cathedral holding a Paternal finger above the plain, and that at the other end should be

Colmar, and that range the Black Forest, and everywhere the apple-red roofs of villages, the white bony spires of their churches accenting the plain) she mused on all that it had meant, and of how the symbolism of what unconsciously one had dismissed as another of the sacred fairy tales of one's childhood, was so simple and obvious that how in the world had it escaped her till now. For she saw it all, standing on a high hill, looking down, and about to turn away. And I will give you all the cities of the earth! So He had stood there, like this, looking down at the distances and turning it over in his mind, knowing that they were afraid and would offer any bribe, and dallying with power and wealth and all its implications. For He was sorely tempted. Only of course they had made it unreal by bringing in the Devil, so that with childhood one outgrew it as one outgrew other childish tales, and years later when one never opened a Bible for months on end (except to prove that it was not Shakespeare) one suddenly saw its undimmed significance. And actually that was all one needed to know about Christ: that and the casting of the first stone. For to the East miracles were nothing new, and prove little except that the masses were the fools then that they are now; and the trial was not more interesting than the trial of Joan of Arc, or the recantation of Galileo, or the excommunication of Spinoza; but the struggle between power and integrity, or gain and conviction, between the retaining and losing of one's essential self, struggle which in greater or lesser degree each carried within himself, *that* they managed somehow to distort for children so that it lay useless and half-remembered as something very noble, very remote, very Guido Reni.

—I'm glad that I'm not rich, said Miss Reade suddenly; forgetting that let alone all the cities of the earth, no one was going to offer her the nearest village unless she got-going and walked to it.

—For I should so loathe to be cluttered-up with possessions, said Miss Reade emphatically. And turned her back on the sunset.

But Sebastian reproved her. One should be more tolerant. One should remember that of all mankind the rich alone enjoyed the privilege of never growing-up. They alone were allowed, without ill consequence to themselves, to remain children all their lives; and might therefore without effort to themselves be dressed and fed and amused. The French must dress and feed them; the Italian provide them with a playground; the Jew with theatres and entertainments. For unlike children in only one particular, they could not provide their own amusement. Therefore the Italian had to let them in his garden, sing to them, and serve their food. The French had to dress and perfume them, and prepare that food. The Jew had to bring them furs, jewels, entertainments, and luxury. To this add the shooting of any bird or beast that was at all swift or graceful, as an excuse for a little lust and exercise.

And just as children who wish to play undisturbed avoid grown-ups who are sure to ask them pertinent questions, so to them the rest of the world was untouchable. Abroad they communicated only with ruins. They shook hands with Museum pieces and patronised the dead Cæsars. (Though not if the effort could be avoided.) For what were trains-de-luxe and Splendide-Splendides but guarantees of isolation? They will travel thousands of miles, only if they are sure of finding their neighbours at their journey's end. They will go only where their neighbours go: possibly to demonstrate to each other that they each have done the same thing. For one must remember they are children. They merely extend the game of hide-and-seek from the nursery to the outside world.

Miss Reade considered this. She said: And do you really make as much money as they say you do, Sebastian?

He reassured her. He also said that if he didn't, he wouldn't work. He said there were only two kinds of writers: those who made money, and those who tried but couldn't. It so happened that he could and did. And had he not been able to do so, he would have given it up long ago and tried his hand at something more lucrative.

At which Miss Reade, who was of a romantic disposition, laughed; convinced that he was teasing her.

Ittswiller (unable to compete with ardent sunsets and proffered cities) proved a dull little anticlimax of a village. But it was all prinked out with flags and bunting, and the children had their heads in curling rags: For to-morrow was a day of days. The new bells were to be consecrated by an imposing, though minor, Bishop.

They found the bells propped on a heavy scaffolding inside the church; very bright and factory-new, and the engraving on their rather pompous stomachs told how in War they had been melted into guns for their country's defence, and how when peace was come again a grateful country gave them back once more to the service of God. This day: this month: this year.

For a while they had stood staring in silence, until Sebastian had said very quietly:

—Having ceased the destruction of the body, they will now resume the destruction of the mind....

Whereupon, in sheer delight, Miss Reade had looked up at him in rueful admiration. But as she could not know the look that lit her face at that moment, she never realised quite how it happened; though once again she was to discover that although the spine may serve some useful purpose, the lips have a disconcerting way of containing most of the essential nerves.

—But this, gasped Miss Reade (whose thoughts but half-an-hour since had been so exalted). But this is a church....

—But there is a carpet on the floor, urged Sebastian, who was very much in earnest.

But there were also footsteps outside. So they wandered

again into the courtyard. Sebastian flushed and extremely annoyed, Miss Reade calm and with confidence in the future. Yet she leaned against the first tree she came to as though her knees were unwilling to support her further; and suddenly looking-up and seeing that it was an apple tree, impulsively picked the first at hand, bit in it, and held it out to him.

For now at last we know, she said, in which season Eve tempted Adam.

He seemed to have been walking a long time and to be always in the same place. Or not so much walking as prowling round an hour that drew no nearer.

In the August heat Paris was its familiar untidy self; very much the French: why should I use a suitcase when string and paper will do as well? Here one might pause mile after mile and never know that anything new existed in the world; old angles, old architecture, old writing of signs, old furniture shops; a gigantic bric-à-brac; Napoleon's writing-table. One walked on through a confusion of Bébé Cadum and Nicholas and scarlet cheeks and cheap (female) scents and shoddy clothes, and grey and white houses against their grey and white clouds, and all the good standing about in the street in the friendly haphazard of a long *marché aux puces* through which one picks a way. For air, that sweetish blend of incense, garlic, drains, and river.

But he had left the river long ago. Hours ago, it seemed, when the thought that three o'clock might come on him unaware and find him far from his objective, miles out of his way, had for a moment made him physically weak with fear so that his hand had trembled as he put back the book he was fingering sightlessly, and had begun walking in the direction he had avoided all the morning. Curious these scruples he had developed, and the sudden protective self-loathing, as certain men develop a physical horror of their wives and feel themselves contaminated each time that resistance is no longer possible. No one seeing his quick step could have guessed the reluctance with which he climbed the steep street, much less have understood his morbid pretence at being in quite a different part of the city. Yet bandage his eyes and he could have passed correctly the butchers' shops with their gilt horses' heads, the rolls of linoleum and strips of cheap carpet, the quincaillerie, the narrow sordid shops spilling their cheap goods on the pavement, the untidy *bistros* with the fly-blown paper on the tables, the sickly beggars. For this was the slope of Menilmontant leading to Père Lachaise, and the first impression had been indelible in that detailed stereoscopic way in which the mind recalls at will the few backgrounds by which it has set store.

And here already was the long stone wall and the side gate he used, for he disdained the imposing main avenue with its steps and ascending cypresses, bronze busts and poetic willow, and trumpery frieze of naked huddled men and women dragging children and the aged after them through an open doorway, and all the other theatrical accessories that tricked it out in a semblance of hope and decency. For was he not an intimate? No sitting in the auditorium for him, who might loiter at will in the wings and lift the curtain on the make-believe.

But now that the wall rose in front of him, Harrion relaxed his step; and as though to drag out still more subtly the pleasures of anticipation, lingered before the last of that dreary array of pokey shops, littered with all the sordid traffic that goes on around the dead; counting again the pots of dusty leaves, the weary bunches of dark leafless flowers (for not a flower that was gay or vital), the beaded wire wreaths of neutral colouring, the trite farewells in enamelled tin of drab design, the whole reminiscent of old serge, of cheerless rooms: a last unlovely echo of their spent lives.

But already the air had a different taste to it; a taste one never forgot, that burnt for hours in mouth and nostrils, so that no smoke is ever afterwards quite the same, even if it is only the burning of leaves in a garden.

An icy moment of panic seized him, till he looked at his wrist and was reassured. It needed twenty minutes to the hour. He turned away from the window and let himself in at the gate with an almost proprietary air of absorbed excitement, passed familiarly between the graves without giving them a glance, and turned down a narrow pathway to the left.

But one of the attendants who saw him coming got up from a bench and came to meet him.

—Le gros-Michel n'est pas là, he whispered. Il est allé casser la croûte.

Harrion stopped; frowned. Would he be back? He would be back; the attendant adding that the ceremony could hardly begin without him, and smiling wanly at his own joke. His was a thin sad face, with rather bleak grey eyes; he pocketed the tip Harrion had pressed in his hand with a curt nod and scarcely a pretence at gratitude (yet he had a wife and three children and could hope for no further promotion for two years at least); watching his benefactor make his quick way in the direction of the Crematorium with something not unlike contempt on his face, and perhaps reflecting that even the gros-Michel, surely the lowest of God's creatures, spat when he spoke of this man.

And Harrion knew perfectly well that he despised him, and that when the attendants saw him they winked at each other, and even that they were a little repelled by the notes he thrust in their expectant palms. But that, if anything, only heightened the exultation that was his the moment he closed the gate behind him and was admitted, however contemptuously, to their midst; for with the shutting of the gate and the attainment, as it were, of his object, all his polite reluctance and self-loathing dropped from him, as though they had been there only to heighten the enjoyment of the moment when it came (at last) after the dreary struggle to put it from him. For here he was a different being. Here once more desire returned to him. Once again life held an interest; an interest that now could never fail and which he shared alone. For here and at last one could love without fear or rebuff Indeed, could be so filled with a love for all mankind as to burn in a glowing heat of ecstasy that made one's footsteps light and suspect as one picked a way between the graves and made oneself not a little ridiculous to the attendants. But that he did not mind. He would not have had it otherwise. He welcomed it. One bore ridicule with humility when one loved humanity as he did. For at last one could love humanity when it suffered as it suffered here. Here, shorn of all its pretence and at its most pitiful; here where all its bitterest tears were shed and its darkest fears went uncomforted. Here where the very air reeked with the stench of man, so that as one took in a breath one drank the flesh and blood of one's fellows in an awful communion of fear and ecstasy. For no sooner was the body on its asbestos mat placed on the altar and the iron doors swung-to, than out of the turret-chimney it rushed, the heavy wave of black and swirling smoke, pouring voluptuously heavenward or forced down to earth like an unwanted sacrifice, and slowly from its dense and angry mass came the aroma of pine-wood as the coffin burnt itself out, then the black smoke thinned and turned to grey and with the change came the subtle retching smell of burning flesh and grease, which in turn changed to a foul penetrating odour of excrement consuming itself, until at last, when one was exhausted and one scarcely could bear more, the grey changed to a thin steady spiral of white, with its acrid taste of burning bone.

But not yet. He looked again at his wrist. It needed still fifteen minutes to the hour. Then the funeral party would arrive, and someone would help the widow or the old people up the steps leading to the Crematorium chapel, and they would disappear, and then his friend the gros-Michel and his men would shoulder the coffin and follow with no more ceremony than if this had been the bringing in of the piano, and still in their blue cotton workmen's blouses, which never failed to call comment from the sad-faced attendant (On dirait des tonneliers! he would murmur indignantly. But then he had a sad face, and scruples, and even after years the sight of weeping widows could still move him to look away), and once the mourners were seated inside the chapel the coffin would be placed on the high curtained altar, and, like a conjurer's best trick, soft music from the organ would be the signal for the drawing-to of the curtains, and from a small trapdoor at the back (but *they* think it all happens here, the gros-Michel had winked at him one day) the coffin would be removed to the furnace-room, and be returned to them later, when the curtains would again be solemnly drawn, as the casket which must be fitted neatly in the walls of the Columbarium outside, with its small marble stones and wall-fitments for a few flowers.

Strange how surprised they always were to see the little box, after the heavy coffin which they had brought there. And what scenes they made, sometimes. As the woman who had come screaming down the steps: My child! My child! Is this all that is left of my child! and crying reproaches at the man with her, who had persuaded her to do this thing.

—But after all, my dear, it is so much cleaner, was all he could find to say in his defence.

O yes one needed a strong stomach for the job, as the pale-faced attendant would emphasize, nodding in the direction of the colossal indifferent Michel and his sturdy assistants. The sad attendant never could hide his disgust of the great hulking jovial red-faced workman who controlled the Crematorium as he the cemetery grounds. For sometimes, the attendant said, the bodies burst their coffins, when they had travelled a long way, for instance, or were the corpses of very fat people in an advanced state of decomposition. Only last month there was that hindou (qu'il était affreux! qu'il était horrible!) whose head had swollen to an enormous size, and the mouth had widened inches outwards across the face and bubbled with a hissing of blood and putrescence. (Bien sûr qu'il faut avoir l'estomac bien placé!) And all the work they got from the hospitals, the abortions, the refuse from the dissecting tables, all arriving pell-mell, human joints, heads, arms, thighs, and to see those great hulking brutes jamming them in the coffins like bits of meat and banging them down with their fists when the lids wouldn't shut. But they were less than men, they were human butchers, they were barbarians. And they've got rubber gloves, too; but do you think they'll use them? And do you think they'll change their filthy clothes after being hours soaked in the smell of decomposition? Try and make them! They go straight out, just as they are, to get a drink. But they won't serve them any more. The barmen say: Get out. It's horrible! Your clothes stink! Still, some-one has got to do it. People do die.

But Harrion was growing restless sitting there on the stone bench in front of the Columbarium and with nothing to do but change his place from one end of it to the other. Whenever he looked up his eye caught the glitter of gold writing on the squares in the nearest walls: *Un bon souvenir de Madeleine. Une bonne pensée. Regrêts. Au-revoir, Joseph.* And the gaps where many a niche had been torn open, as were some of the graves outside. Their payments, then, had lapsed. That was what it meant: For five years they could have the few inches, the few feet, then out of consideration (for the survivors were not all neglectful, but might be ill or in momentary financial difficulties) the grave or urn was left another year. But after that, no more. The bones were tipped in the *fosse communal* and there the matter ended. There was no appeal, no redress. Pick them out, if you can. For again the wealthy were in their palaces and the poor were in their tenements. And again the poor could not pay the rent and suffered the Ultimate Eviction. My dear Sir, my dear Madam, the rent is due. We regret, but. Out you go. For he must pay rent all his life and his bones must pay rent, or they, too, shall not rest in peace. Not even rest in his length of earth, nor stop a seven-inch hole in a wall. Even that is not conceded man in his last abject attempt at privacy. But there is humanity in the deed. They will not throw his bones out in the street as when he was alive. Nor will they scatter them, as he might have hoped, to the impartial winds. For human bones must be respected and may not be thrown heedlessly away. They may be thrown only in the public ossuary. So get out. We are sorry. But we need this room. Get out. Shuffle your bones with the least of your fellows, with the unknown, and the unloved, and the forgotten.

But how little all that mattered, Harrion was thinking (at last one could love humanity when it suffered like this, at its most pitiful, at its most desolate!) for the last flame goes up from the brain. From the brain, not from the heart. Though he hadn't believed it, until they had proved it to him. But when at last the grey column of smoke ascending the air grew barely perceptible, and the tang of burning bone began to die away, and all flesh consumed, the framework of bone lay in cinders on its asbestos mat, then the heart and the brain ran their last macabre race, ironically staging their last fight over a victim long past caring. And when the doors were opened and the mat drawn out with its bright calcinous trail, only the brain burned on in its burst shell of skull. For at the end, it seemed, man's inconstant heart must bow down before his spirit, the last white flame to leave the body.

Less than five minutes now. Should he stay where he was when the funeral drove up, or go indoors in the furnace-room? But he had been too often behind the scenes, lately. Michel was growing annoyed, and even an extra large tip had not stopped him grumbling yesterday, when, as he said, there had been nothing to see, rien que des fœtus et des nouveau-né sent from the maternity hospitals, and for that he'd probably lose his job, if all this got about. Even though (thought Harrion) he couldn't be seen, standing there behind the furnace with his eyes glued to the mica opening for as long as the heat was bearable. How unreal it was the way the whole thing swayed and split, sizzling like fat that has caught fire in a frying-pan, and the maddened gathering of the roaring cataract of flame as the light pine covering burst away and then like two fiery swords cutting it up, the flames fastened on the flesh. Sometimes Michel would prod the body like an enormous sausage, turning it over with a curse, if it were that of a very fat person that wouldn't burn quickly enough. (So the pale attendant said, with disgust. He hadn't seen that yet.) But once he had been allowed to scoop the bones into the urn with the long wire brush, and watch them grow cold after all the fury and recede from fiery red to an indifferent grey.

But this must be the funeral. A carriage was drawing up. And there was Michel and his men coming down the steps. (Then he had been there all the time, and hadn't let him know!) And now he was pretending not to see him. It was quite obvious that he was pretending not to see him, as he sat there on the bench trying to ask by signs whether he might come or not. Still, he must use tact. He mustn't anger him.

The mourners in the first coach, Harrion noticed, were anything but sorrowful. Particularly the men, who seemed to have drunk rather more than was wise and were grinning together and cracking jokes. Their women, sitting at the back, pursed their lips resentfully at their fun, and seemed not to be enjoying this part of the afternoon at all. They didn't care, he reflected. They wouldn't mind. They might even say: yes, come along! Still, he must be patient. Another day would do as well. Now the coffin was being lifted from the hearse. Now it was being carried up the steps. And still no one looked round at him. The door shut with a bang.

And with the shutting of the door, he had (he always had) a spasm of self-loathing, a longing to get away. And again resistance made him sick and excited, till he felt his stomach dragged down as though falling out of his body. But to-day he would stay where he was. Nothing should move him. No; he'd shut his eyes. No; that was not enough. He must go away. He must go now, before it began. To-day he would be strong. He would leave before it could overpower him.

With the suddenness of an explosion the column of black smoke rushed up from the furnace chimney, mounted, wavered, and swept down to the ground, away from him, on the opposite side of the Columbarium.

Then the wind was in the north to-day. He should have thought of that. He hadn't realised. He leapt up and, breathing hard, reached the other side, only just in time, it seemed to him. He leaned against a pillar to steady himself, with nostrils distended like an animal flaring the scent of another; and it came surprisingly quickly after the black burning of the wood, the thin grey column in ascension perpetual with its stench of grease and putrescence. He smiled, and held up his face.

From a height the sun chose, drowsy fastidious bee, now this village, now that.

—There is a future for these people, Sebastian was saying.

And Lavinia Reade, shading her eyes from the bright look of the day, and gazing down at the bacchic frieze of grapes, the tumbling children and burdened fields, and oxen remote in their unhurried condescension, said: No! There is an eternity.

Founded in 1986, Serpent's Tail publishes the innovative and the challenging.

If you would like to receive a catalogue of our current publications please write to:

FREEPOST
Serpent's Tail
4 Blackstock Mews
LONDON N4 2BR

(No stamp necessary if your letter is posted in the United Kingdom.)

Also published as an Extraordinary Classic by Serpent's Tail

The Book of Disquiet
Fernando Pessoa
Translated by Margaret Jull Costa

'Not the least beautiful aspect of this exquisite artist's output is his patent indifference to fame and praise, hiding as he does behind imagined personalities. Of course Bernardo Soares is expressing Pessoa's concerns, which are often mordant and despairing; yet the fictional distance allows the reader to acknowledge that a seemingly dull bookkeeper, confronted daily with rows of figures, can have an inner life of unexpected richness . . . This book has moved me more than anything I have read in years.'   PAUL BAILEY in *The Daily Telegraph*

'This central figure of European modernism has been very badly served by English translations, so it was a real bonus when Serpent's Tail published *The Book of Disquiet*, a meandering, melancholic series of reveries and meditations, ostensibly written by one Bernardo Soares, a lugubrious office clerk in 1930's Lisbon.'

WILLIAM BOYD's 'Book of the Year' in the *TLS*

'It could not have been written in England; there is too much thought racing hopelessly around. The elegance of the style, well conveyed in what seems to be a more than adequate translation, is an important component and a very ironic one . . . There is a distinguished mind at work beneath the totally acceptable dullness of clerking. The mind is that of Pessoa. We must be given the chance to learn more about him.'

ANTHONY BURGESS in *The Observer*

Also published as an Extraordinary Classic by Serpent's Tail

The Shipyard
Juan Carlos Onetti
Translated by Nick Caistor

'Issued in a weird and wonderful series simply called Extraordinary Classics, this is the Kafkaesque story of a man who takes up a post as the general manager of a defunct and rotten shipyard ... The novel is entirely free from parable or pretention and Onetti's superb feel for casual, down-at-heel urban atmosphere makes it a totally three-dimensional exploration of the landscape of quiet despair.'
The Sunday Times

'Many Latin-American novelists have been called in the last thirty years, but few have made trumps with English readers. On the evidence of *The Shipyard*, Juan Carlos Onetti deserves to be among the few ... Is it a one-off masterpiece? I hope that, having reconstituted *The Shipyard* for English readers, the translator and publisher will decide to take the rust off the rest of Onetti's works.'
The Spectator

'In times of economic hardship for progressive publishers, it is a brave and determined body that carries on. One such is Serpent's Tail, which manages to produce books of originality and beauty while many other houses fail ...
Onetti's achievement in *The Shipyard* is a unique one. His world is one peopled by phantoms, yet his characters are solid—forged and mis-shapen by the hell that is their lives "back from having been nowhere".
Yet bankruptcy, fraud and exploitation are also at the centre of Onetti's story, and the forces of the real world give its grotesquerie a grim and unremitting truth.'
Morning Star

Also published as an Extraordinary Classic by Serpent's Tail

The Walk
Robert Walser
Translated by Christopher Middleton and others

'Robert Walser is one of the important German-language writers of this century... [He is] a Paul Klee in prose—as delicate, as sly, as haunted. A cross between Stevie Smith and Beckett: a good-humoured, sweet Beckett. And as literature's present inevitably remakes its past, so we cannot help but see Walser as the missing link between Kleist and Kafka, who adored him greatly... Walser's virtues are those of the most mature, most civilized art. He is a truly wonderful, heart-breaking writer.' SUSAN SONTAG.

'If he had a hundred thousand readers, the world would be a better place.' HERMANN HESSE

'His deep and instinctive distaste for everything... that has rank and privilege, makes him an essential writer of our time...' ELIAS CANETTI

'Many of these pieces have a didactic feel to them, but it's hard to lose sight of his humorous manner, sometimes cheeky petulance and mock-solemnic syntax. Walser was an influence on Franz Kafka and it's not difficult to see how.' *Northern Star*

'If you look on this collection of short stories as an opportunity to take a series of literary strolls, as though for a breath of fresh air, you would be right and wrong at the same time. Despite their brevity and apparent clarity they are much, much deeper, as was Robert Walser. If you fathom the meaning behind them you could be enervated by your stroll.' *The Vale*